Scattered Lights

Steve Wiegenstein

ISBN: 978-0-578-73780-5

Library of Congress Control Number: 2020943171

Designed by Phillip Howerton and by Ronald Kerns of StudioKerns.

Special thanks to assistant editor Morgan Blanck.

Cover photograph: *Evening Light on the Briscoe Porch*

Cornerpost Press
214 West Maple
West Plains, Missouri 65775
www.cornerpostpress.com

Acknowledgements

Grateful acknowledgment is given to the publications in which some of these stories first appeared.

The End of the World
Kansas Quarterly

Why Miss Elizabeth Never Joined the Shakespeare Club
Louisiana Literature

Trio Sonata in C
Southern Humanities Review

From Thee to My Sole Self
Jumping Pond: Poems and Stories from the Ozarks

The Trouble with Women
Oxford Magazine

Bill Burkens and Peter Krull
Beloit Fiction Journal

Magic Kids
Elder Mountain

Signs and Wonders
The Nebraska Review

To the friends, neighbors, family members, loved ones, mentors, tormentors, classmates, weirdos, roughnecks, role models, nitwits, objects of admiration, church members, co-workers, troublemakers, peacemakers, ancestors, companions, irritants, and fellow sojourners who have helped to make me the person and the writer that I am, this book is lovingly dedicated.

My instinct tells me that my head is an organ for burrowing, as some creatures use their snout and fore-paws, and with it I would mine and burrow my way through these hills. I think that the richest vein is somewhere hereabouts; so by the divining-rod and thin rising vapors I judge; and here I will begin to mine.

Henry David Thoreau, *Walden*

Contents

The End of the World

Larry works at the Dixie Food Mart. Though it is the smaller of the two grocery stores in Piedmont, everyone agrees that it has the best produce department. At the Dixie Food Mart the fruits and vegetables glisten shamelessly, begging to go home with you. Tiny droplets of water cling to the leaf lettuce, the oranges, the green peppers, everything; the place is a rain forest, it is a botanical garden. As you pass through, making your selections, Larry follows behind and rearranges the displays so there are no gaps. The next customer sees the same virginal rows of shining food.

Larry neither smokes nor drinks. He is single, thirty years old.

Larry has always lived in Piedmont. He neither likes nor dislikes the town. He thinks about it the way an air bubble thinks about water; it is a transparent medium within which he moves, and without which he would be inconceivable.

Larry lives in Hillwood Terrace, the trailer park out on Highway 34, in a nice little sixty-footer. He awakens at 4:30, usually a few seconds before his alarm is about to go off, in order to clock in by 5:30. After he has dressed and eaten breakfast, he likes to sit on the mesh-steel steps of his trailer and say his morning prayers. If it is raining or cold, he says them at the kitchen table.

Larry believes the end of the world is at hand, for all the signs are in place and the corruption of the world has grown so great that the Lord will surely not stand its stench much longer. The end of the world is a regular subject of his morning prayers; he asks the Lord to let it come soon.

Why not today? Larry asks the Lord this morning, sitting in the dark on the steps of his trailer. Why not today? He waits for a long moment to see if the voice of the Holy Spirit might reply. Then he goes back inside to wash his skillet, plate, knife, and fork. The silence of the trailer oppresses him, and he begins to whistle.

Larry clocks in three minutes late, not enough to matter much but a nuisance nevertheless. The assistant produce manager, whose name is Bus, is already there, but is hung over and has not begun work on the morning's displays. Bus is only a couple of years out of high school; he is small and thin, with acne and long blond hair. He twitches his head backward every few seconds to keep the hair from falling into his eyes. In his bow tie and apron, he looks like a delinquent dressed up to impress a judge.

"I feel like shit soup," Bus says in greeting.

"Aren't you the charmer," Larry replies.

Stacking onions with Bus, Larry lets one get away. It rolls against a refrigerated counter, and when Larry bends to retrieve it, some of his tracts fall out of his apron pocket and onto the floor. Larry keeps two sets of tracts in his pocket: *Is There a Hell?* for the unbelievers, *What Jesus Really Meant* for the doctrinally confused.

"You're gonna get in trouble doing that Baby Jesus bit in the store again," Bus says.

"I'm not going to bother anybody. That's all he told me. He just said not to bother anybody."

Mr. Brooks owns the Dixie Food Mart. He is a large man, fleshy, balding, hairy-armed, quick to sweat, the kind of man we imagine keeling over unexpectedly with a burst blood vessel in the brain, shocking the town. He has a wife, whose name is Arlene, and a teenage daughter, whose name is Tami and who is causing him great worry these days. Bus has confided to Larry that Tami is top-rank hot stuff.

"I went out with her one time," Bus said, waving his hand in the air as if to cool a burn. "Man alive."

"I don't want to hear your smutty talk," said Larry.

"I heard she took on these two guys from the basketball team."

"I *said*—"

"Yeah, I bet you don't."

Mr. Brooks has partially assuaged his worry by making Tami work at the Food Mart after school and during the summer; she is a good checker, fast and accurate. But still there are the nights and weekends, and Mr. Brooks can only watch and fret.

Another worry for Mr. Brooks is the prospect of having to fire Larry. Passing the produce department one day some months ago, he noticed Larry talking intensely to Mrs. Briscoe, a good customer and a friend of Arlene's. Larry pressed a tract into her hand; she pushed it back at him. Mr. Brooks confiscated the tracts and told Larry never to bring them to work again. He suspects that Larry is disobeying, but he also loves the way the produce department looks. Sales have been good. Customers have been switching from the Shop 'n' Save.

Mr. Brooks does not believe the end of the world is at hand. He is a Methodist and confines his cosmological speculations to the whereabouts of his daughter.

Larry loves to contemplate the Rapture. Two will be laboring in the field; one will be taken and one will be left. Two will be grinding at the mill; one will be taken and one will be left. Husbands will grope in the night for vanished wives; telephones will ring and ring and ring and ring; grocery store owners will wait in vain for their produce managers to arrive. Empty automobiles careening across the highway, empty airplanes plunging through the sky. A single onion, bouncing once on the hard tile floor of the Dixie Food Mart, will make a strangely loud sound as it drops from an absent hand.

Larry is kept busy most of the morning. The lettuce has been getting poor lately; he has to field complaints. Larry always tries to listen very carefully to what the customer has to say and then give a friendly, but accurate, answer, and for this reason he is often distressed when the customer merely tosses out a remark without staying around to hear Larry's reply.

When his turn comes to go on break, he retreats to the small office area he has fixed up for himself in the back. Bus has been sitting in Larry's chair smoking cigarettes again; there are ashes all over the floor and the air is foul and stale.

That was the third time this month. Mr. Brooks would have to be told.

Giving Bus a glare as he marches through the produce department toward the cash registers, Larry marshals his arguments. The smell getting into the boxes of vegetables stacked nearby. The fire hazard. The fact, though this was an argument meant only for himself, that Bus was a smart-acting kid who didn't deserve the consideration he had already gotten and was now abusing.

Mr. Brooks is standing in the courtesy booth at the front of the store. In the raised, glassed-in cubicle, he looks like something on display—a zoo animal, a special purchase—as he tries to talk on the phone and cash someone's check at the same time. Larry stops and pretends to straighten up the spice shelves as he watches Mr. Brooks, hearing him say, "Now, honey . . . "

It is clearly not the time to bring up Bus and his cigarettes. Mr. Brooks has not been himself lately, somehow; he seems distracted and careworn. He would probably just shrug off another complaint, no matter how justified. Larry feels sorry for him and returns to the produce department.

"I want you to quit using my office for your cancer breaks," he tells Bus when he gets the opportunity. "Do your smoking outside."

"What office?"

"You know what office."

"That's a chair. An office is a place with like a door and your name on the door. When you get an office, and it has like 'Baby

Jesus' in big letters on the door, I promise I'll never smoke in it."
Bus puckers as if to throw him a kiss.

Larry has split with the Victory Assembly and joined the Holy Fellowship Temple in a dispute over Christian perfectionism, whether being born again could enable a person to become entirely free from sin, the Assembly taking the negative viewpoint and the Fellowship the positive. Both groups had their scriptural citations; Larry studied them for weeks. But as he was praying one morning, Larry heard the Lord's answer.

"The soul is my perfect, glorious jewel," it told him. "Join the Holy Fellowship." So he did.

At lunch, Tami comes back to the produce department looking fierce, her high school yearbook, *The Palimpsest*, in her hand. "Where is that shit who works with you?" she says to Larry. Her voice is high and barely under control, although she tries to make it sound comical. "I want to see the little shit."

Bus is nowhere to be seen.

"Look at what he did," she says.

The Dixie Food Mart, as usual, had taken out a full-page ad in the yearbook, and Tami had been getting autographs from the employees: To a Good Co-Worker, From Mrs. Hall; To My Freind Tammy, Have A Good Life, Wally. In the lower left corner is Bus's autograph:

> To Tami,
> A real "Fun" gal
> who I wish I could of
> got to "Know Better"!
> But thanks for the hand
> job anyway.
>   Bus

"Do you know what my dad will do if he sees this? I'll be stuck at home for life." She stares up at Larry as if he were to blame for something. Larry can't meet the quantity of rage in her stare, so he looks away, embarrassed. The image of Bus and Tami in a car somewhere appears before him, unwanted; he tries to chase it away.

Tami seems to read his thoughts. "I only did it because he whined and begged. The little shit."

The last "shit" had quavered, risen, been cut off early; Tami is about to cry, right there in the empty aisle of his beautiful produce department, in her bright red apron and ironic Green Day T-shirt. Larry takes the yearbook out of her hands and plucks a pen from her apron pocket. He whispers, as if a sudden sound might jar loose a landslide of vegetables.

"Can I sign it?"

She watches him, her face rigid, her eyes puffy and suspicious. Larry has never looked her in the face before; she is pretty beneath her clumsy makeup. He writes, "To a real sweet girl and a good checker," and signs it, studying the ink. It is the same color as Bus's signature, a standard issue Dixie Food Mart pen, no doubt. He reexamines Bus's message. Right after "hand" he writes, "in getting me this" in his best Bus-imitation scribble and hands back the book.

Larry had dated a girl named Connie in high school, and one night they tried to have sex in the back of his car. It was a failure, with Larry squirting semen over the seat, her legs, and himself. "What happened?" Connie said. "Am I frigid or something?"

Larry had stopped seeing her. He had long since repented of the sin and prayed for forgiveness. After graduation, Connie had moved to St. Louis, married a man who worked at the Chrysler plant, and had three kids. Still, sometimes he imagined himself at the bar of judgment. Pages would be turned in a huge, living book, and there would be Connie, sixteen, ruined, foolish, her nose squashed down by his naked shoulder.

Tami studies the yearbook, strolling down the aisle toward the dairy case. Larry follows, feeling hungry, although he has just finished lunch. He pushes his hands in his pockets.

Finally she stops. "This is good," she says. "This is amazing. You're a genius."

Larry watches her pick up a bag of carrots and turn it over and over, peering through the orange plastic. She is wearing blue jeans. Larry reminds himself that he does not approve of pants on women.

"My dad always said you were smart," she says. "He talks about you."

"What does he say?"

"Mmmm." Tami looks up at him, smiles. "You're not supposed to ask." She has a chipped front tooth. Larry gazes at it. Ordinarily he does not like imperfections, but the more he studies her tooth the more he likes it. It is a flaw that organizes her face; the rest of her features arrange themselves around it and are made more attractive. It gives Tami's smile a look of homespun honesty that is missing from all those phony billboard beauties. It makes her look unique.

Reading his mind again, Tami asks, "Do you believe in love at first sight?" She glances past him.

"Well, no," Larry says, and then regrets it.

"I've been reading a book called *Love at First Sight*. It's a romance novel. The people in it fall in love at first sight."

He tries to think of something to say. He looks down at the yearbook in her hands; she is a senior, which means she must be seventeen or eighteen. "Listen, I'd like to——"

She stands there. Larry wonders: Like to what? Bus's phrase, "top-rank hot stuff," returns to him, and an image of her, carnal and glorious, flits through his unhappy mind.

"Do you ever go to church?" he asks. An expression—annoyance, petulance, sadness?—crosses her face like the shadow of a cloud passing over a lake.

"I don't know. Pretty boring." She laughs for an instant, as if to soften the remark, and chews on her little finger.

"Oh, no," Larry says. "It's not boring at all. You just have to listen for the message. There's a lot of—you know, a lot of—"

She walks farther down the aisle. "Well, I don't know." Larry stays beside her, licking his lips.

"Do you have a church?" he says.

"Sure. Kind of."

"I mean a *real* church." Tami studies the cheese. "A lot of churches these days, they're just social clubs. People go there to make *contacts*." He says the word with a sneer. It is happening too fast. "They forget what they're there for—to save their souls, to turn their lives around."

Tami turns away toward the checkout lanes. Gently, he holds her wrist and brings out a copy of *What Jesus Really Meant*. "I'd like you to have this. Really. I think the Lord wants you to have it." He tucks the pamphlet into the breast pocket of her apron, and the hairs on his hand prickle as he feels the flesh beneath.

A movement at the other end of the aisle catches his eye. It is Mr. Brooks, who for some reason has left the courtesy booth and come out into the aisles. Tami disappears toward the registers, and Larry is alone.

Mr. Brooks waves him into the storage room, breathing in short loud puffs. He rubs his meaty palm across his face.

"Let's see what you've got there."

Larry hands him a tract. Mr. Brooks glances at it and tucks it into his coat pocket.

"You know what I told you."

Larry looks at Mr. Brooks's sport coat. It is badly worn, slick-looking. It has a stain just below the breast pocket. Mr. Brooks needs to get a new sport coat. The store has an image to maintain. Sure, Piedmont is a small town, and people put up with a lot, but still—

The room is cold but his feet feel hot. Mr. Brooks's voice drones on.

Now was the time for the end of the world to come. Trumpets, trumpets, thunder, clouds. Please, Larry thinks, please. Don't let me lose my job. At the same time, he recognizes that the world is not going to end just to save him from embarrassment; he feels ashamed of himself for even asking.

But still—

What better time? Why not now?

"So here's what I'm going to do," Mr. Brooks says. "First, I want you to give me your solemn promise that you will never bring those things into the store again. And I do mean solemn promise. Can you do that?"

Larry has always appreciated the story of Simon Peter, who turned chicken once things got rough. He understands how Peter must have loathed himself when his human instincts got the better of his spiritual ones, sending him sneaking through the city: Don't know the guy. Never heard of him.

Still, Peter had recovered himself in time and had gone on to great accomplishments; Larry doubts whether he ever could. He fears that once he loses his guts, he will never get them back. So he has volunteered for the witnessing groups again and again, trying to build up his ability to stand up for Jesus in any situation. One evening a week he drives through the countryside around Piedmont, stopping at every house to leave tracts and witness to the unsaved. He draws dots on a map of the county; red for *Beat it*, blue for *Come back some other time*, green for *Yes, I'm interested*. There aren't many green dots.

He hates most of all the walk from his car to the door. He knows what kind of figure he cuts in his suit and tie, a small scrawny man with a Bible in one hand and a bundle of tracts in the other; he feels exposed, ridiculous. People shout through the door for him to go away. Once he came to a house in the early evening. Through the front window he could see a man—a huge man, gigantically fat, with crewcut gray hair, dressed in a white shirt and white pants— sitting on the sofa, watching *Jeopardy*. The man gave no response to Larry's knock. The contestants were crying out in crisp, confident voices.

"Sir?" Larry called. The man made no move until a commercial break came. Then he turned his head ponderously, like a bison. They looked at each other in silence. "Sir?" Larry called again.

They gazed at one another. The show resumed, and the man turned his head away.

Larry backed off the porch and ran to his car. His stomach felt queasy. He felt as though he had seen a personal vision of death.

As the years had gone by, Larry thought that perhaps his visitation trips were helping him, that he was becoming a more robust soldier for the Lord. But standing before Mr. Brooks, he knows that he is no better than before; he is going to cave in without a murmur. He looks into himself and finds that this realization does not surprise him.

"Yes, I promise." That was easy, Larry thinks.

"Second, I'm giving you tomorrow off. Stay home and get all this holy-rolling out of your system. Understand?"

Larry nods.

"And if you mess around with this on Food Mart time again, you're fired on the spot. Got that?"

He nods again.

"Say it out loud. I want you to say it aloud."

"I understand." Larry's cheeks burn.

Mr. Brooks leans against a stack of lettuce crates. He takes a quarter out of his pocket and holds it up between them.

"You know the old render-unto-Caesar," he says. "This is Caesar's palace, Larry. You've rendered yourself unto Caesar for eight hours plus lunch. Outside of here you do what you please. But in here—"

He tosses the quarter to Larry. "Now go home."

Washing his face in the employees' restroom, Larry catches a glimpse in the mirror: Bus peeking around a pile of empty boxes.

"Did you tell him?" Larry shouts. "Did you tell?"

Bus leans out from behind the boxes but doesn't come any closer. "Every baby Jesus gotta have his baby Judas."

"Well, you can't have my job yet. I'm not fired."

Driving home, he is filled with indifference. His soul is not the Lord's pure, perfect jewel, and never will be. He watches the trees and houses and pastures slide past his window. Let it come now, the end of the world, and destroy him along with the rest of the world's rot and corruption. Let it rain sulfur. Let Tami burn. Let Mr. Brooks burn. The earth itself would spout fire, the rivers spout fire. Houses would burn. Let them. Let the forests burn. Let the cities burn. Let the lakes burn. Let the rivers burn. Let the cattle burn, and the horses and the deer and birds and dogs and babies. Let it all burn.

Weeds and Wildness

Everybody knew Charley Blankenship to be something of a loose cannon, a man you didn't want to get into an argument with at a ball game or a bar, because you truly never knew what Charley might do: swing a log chain, poison your dog, or drunkenly hug you and declare that you were right, after all. Mark was in the same class as one of the Blankenship boys, John Wayne, and they shared a spot at the end of the bench during basketball games. So he knew Charley a little from his occasional visits to games, where he would lean over the bench behind them and say, "You got this, boys. That bunch ain't worth shit except that one dude. Put a couple of you defensive specialists on him and they wouldn't score thirty."

"Defensive specialist" was a charitable phrase for someone who never made the linescore except during blowouts, and Mark had always figured that Charley's appearances were his way of letting his son know he was there, supporting him, since he wouldn't have much opportunity to cheer if he waited until they were in a game. Coach always called them "Salt 'n' Pepa" in a lame attempt at coachly humor, since although the two were both average height and average build, Mark was pale and freckled while John Wayne, like his father, had a thick wave of black hair, like a Fifties rock 'n' roll star, and a steady growth of facial hair that seemed entirely inappropriate for a high school student. They knew that their real resemblance was in the fact that they would never get in a game that mattered. Still, a dad hovering behind the bench was an embarrassment. John Wayne remained studiously neutral until his dad returned to the bleachers, and then the two of them would exchange a glance of hard-boiled, high-school-boy sympathy.

So Charley was a character. Everybody in town knew him. But no one expected it when the ATF people swooped in and arrested him, with a helicopter and a line of cars that sped through town at four in the morning. On the courthouse lawn they spread out the haul for the cameras: belts of ammunition, grenades and grenade launchers, and the centerpiece of the raid, a .50-caliber machine gun that had somehow walked away from Fort Leonard Wood about a year ago.

By then it was the spring of senior year, and nobody knew what to say to John Wayne. For although the cache had been found in a locked shed at the far end of the Blankenship property, and although Charley's lawyer insisted that things were not all as they appeared, it was only natural to infer that John Wayne knew what was going on. But no charges were ever brought, John Wayne continued attending classes, and Charley wound up taking a plea deal that sent him to the federal prison in Forrest City, Arkansas, not too far a drive for weekend visits.

Mark's dad preached at the First Baptist Church, on the west edge of town, and, as the pastor of a respectable church, knew that the subject was off limits. There was ample room to talk about sin and error, repentance, and redemption, without getting into local matters. But Grandpa, who still lived on the old place down by the river, didn't mince words when he came in for Sunday dinner.

"The Blankenships have been getting more foolish with every generation," he said. "Charley is the worst of the bunch. But at least he didn't peach on his boy, and I give him credit for that."

After graduation, John Wayne went into the service, as he had planned since sophomore year, but before leaving he told everyone that he wanted to be called just Wayne from here on out. He didn't specify whether he was tired of the association with the old cowboy movie star, whether he had figured out that "John Wayne" was the name of too many criminals to count, or whether he wanted to disassociate himself from anything his father had given him. But

Wayne it was, so all the news tidbits that the Army sent home called him "Wayne Blankenship": his completion of basic training, his attainment of specialist status, his marksmanship badge, his deployment overseas.

Mark didn't know what to do with himself. The military had no appeal. Coach liked to berate him during practice that he lacked the killer instinct, the one quality that kept him off the starting five. "Looky there," he would say, pointing to Dwayne Jackson at the other end of the court, strutting like a banty after knocking down another of his patented shots from the corner. "The only thing that separates you from him is Dwayne's got the killer instinct." Mark didn't doubt that one bit, having been punched out in the dressing room by Dwayne more times than he cared to think. And presumably Wayne was off acquiring the killer instinct, or its near relative. But Mark didn't want to have the killer instinct. He wanted to live a harmless life, an existence like a bee or a flower, a lily of the field like in the verse Dad preached on whenever he conducted the funeral of a little old lady nobody could remember anything about.

College, the other obvious option. His friends were going off to SEMO or Missouri State, or the community college or the tech school, and there were scholarships at Southwest Baptist for the children of clergy, a tidbit that his parents dropped into conversation weekly. But Mark felt worn out with quizzes and exams, required readings, the whole machinery of education that had been grinding away for the last dozen years. He wanted to stop thinking for a while, to simply live, without the urgency of preparing himself for something yet to come. So he dawdled and delayed, and he missed deadlines for applying, until he had procrastinated himself into a semester of nothing.

That left work. The Farm & Home Supply was hiring, and the manager, a parishioner, took his application without a glance and told him to show up on Monday. "We'll get you a name tag fixed up," he said. "Wear a clean shirt with a collar. No dirt or stains. Minimum wage for the first six months."

"Yes, sir," Mark said.

The manager paused and looked up. "You come from good people. That means a lot around here. A lot of kids, they want to shake the dust from off their feet as soon as school's over, but if you stick around, you can make a good life for yourself. Ten years ago, I came out of high school and took a job here, stocking shelves and running the register. There's a future in rural supply."

"Yes, sir," Mark repeated, feeling foolish that he could think of nothing else to say. But the manager didn't appear to notice, and after they shook hands Mark stood blinking in the sunlight outside, struck with the sudden impulse to call Grandpa. He picked up on the second ring, which probably meant that he had been napping.

"I'm in the parking lot of the Farm & Home. Anything you need?"

The pause at the other end of the line told him that Grandpa was trying to figure out his reason for calling, since Mark rarely ran errands unprompted and Grandpa usually took care of his own tasks. Mark would have told him that he felt adrift and lonesome, that everyone was moving on ahead of him, and that he needed to be around someone who conveyed a sense of calm about the uncertain future ahead. But they were not people who spoke of such things, although Mark imagined that Grandpa could sense it.

"Maybe. How much they want for a roll of woven wire?"

"I'll go check." He kept the call open as he walked to the side of the building, where the large items were stacked. "Hundred and fifty dollars."

"That's about right." But he didn't ask for a roll, since they both knew that Mark wouldn't have that kind of money in his pocket or anywhere near.

"If you can wait till next week, I can get you the employee discount."

"Is that right? You gonna work there? Come on out and tell me about it."

That was the invitation Mark had been angling for. He checked himself in the rear-view mirror, for Grandpa did not approve of disheveled young people, and headed down the county road toward the river.

Grandpa still lived on his old place, the home place as Dad called it, although it was really time for him to move to town. He didn't farm any more but rented out the pasture to the neighbors, who took care of the haying and fences. So he puttered around the house and barn, and he worked as a caretaker at the Nature Camp up the road, run by a charity from St. Louis that brought kids down to experience the outdoors. The Nature Camp consisted of a cluster of cabins a few hundred yards down from where the steel truss bridge crossed the river, a fine old barn where they kept their horses and tack, and a big stone assembly hall, supposedly over a hundred years old, that they used for meals and evening programs. Grandpa kept their buses running and their pathways mowed, and in the off-season he served as an unofficial security guard, shooing away teenagers and calling the sheriff on more significant intruders.

As a boy, Mark occasionally rode over to it with his grandfather, and he was always struck to see how they greeted him with casual friendliness and childish enthusiasm, the staffers waving with "Hi, Ott" and the campers dashing over to filch Jolly Ranchers out of his pocket as he patted their heads. To Mark, Grandpa had always been loved but a little scary, a man with neatly combed gray hair and black-rimmed eyeglasses who looked like the picture of Barry Goldwater in his history book, someone who stood at the peak of deference and respect. But to these people he was a kindly old man with a toolbox, one of the locals, and little more. He was a different person to them, someone inconsequential, and strangest of all, he didn't seem to mind. He had caught Mark's eye once as he filled his pockets with the candies he kept in a canister on top of the refrigerator. "Those kids don't have the advantages we do," he said. "I always like to give them a little sport."

Grandpa sat on the front porch waiting for him, two glasses of iced tea on the table, as he pulled in the lane. "There's the working man," he said. Mark took the other porch chair beside him.

"Your mom and dad were hoping you'd pull the trigger at the last minute and sign up for college," Grandpa said. "Even some classes up at Flat River."

"I just didn't feel ready. Maybe in January."

"There's many an honorable thing a man can do without a college degree, and just as many dishonorable things to do without one. I only made it out of high school through the charity of a couple of teachers. You do what you think is right."

Mark sipped his tea, feeling inward relief. Everyone else had been free with their opinions on what he should do with the rest of his life, and he was happy not to have to go through it one more time.

"I want to ask your help on something, now that you're going to be around here for a while," Grandpa said.

"Sure."

"I can't do some of the work at the Nature Camp anymore, or if I do it, I have to spend the next day resting up. I thought maybe you could help me out a little."

"Of course."

"Thanks. Let's run up there and look things over. Perfect timing, they're between sessions so no kids around. I already told the director I'd be asking you for help."

Grandpa kept an old golf cart in the driveway for short runs, so they climbed in and hummed up the road to the Nature Camp, through the elaborate gate, and past the main office, where the director waved from the door. "My grandson!" he shouted over the whir of the electric motor as they rode through the double row of cabins to the assembly hall, which stood on a slope above the rest of the camp, halfway to the edge of the woods. Behind the assembly hall stood a nondescript shed.

"This is where I keep my equipment," Grandpa said, stopping the cart and climbing out. "I'll get you a key."

From this high spot, they could see all the way down the valley: the residential cabins, the archery and rifle range against the hillside, the craft and nature cabins halfway between. Farther south, the pool, tennis courts, and horse barn, and beyond it in the distance, Grandpa's place. The county road glistened black in the sunshine, its asphalt starting to soften, and across the road they could see the river, where the children were not allowed to swim even if they wanted to. Too many hidden hazards beneath the surface, roots and rocks waiting to rear up into a lawsuit. Across the river, he knew but could not see, was Charley Blankenship's place a couple of miles up the road, at the end of a long, rutted lane that he never graded, using poor maintenance as a tool for privacy.

Mark had never seen the valley from this vantage before. "It's like a little town all its own," he murmured.

"So it is," Grandpa said. "Used to be one, too. There was a whole settlement here in the old days, post office and everything."

"What happened to it?"

"What happens to all human things? One generation passeth away, and another generation cometh." He pointed up the hill behind them to a little graveyard at the edge of the woods with a chain-link fence around it. "Nobody ever comes to visit that place anymore, but I like to keep it cleaned up, just because." Unlike Dad, Grandpa didn't pause to sermonize. "That's one thing I want you to do—run the weedeater. I do fine on the riding mower, but after a day trimming weeds, I'm about busted." His gesture took in the whole operation. "I start up here at the cemetery and work down. Don't go to the horse barn, though. The horse people like to do things their own way, and they get huffy if you mess with their territory."

Mark had a hard time imagining himself running the trimmer for an entire day but knew he would have to if he wanted to keep up with his grandfather. He was a man of the older generation, for whom the only choices were to work until the job was done or work until you keeled over.

"All right," he said. "No trimming down by the horse barn."

Grandpa pointed to the residential cabins. "Some of those need a new coat of paint. I've been meaning to get to them but don't trust myself on a ladder nowadays. Maybe you can do the high and I can do the low."

Mark began to regret agreeing to this task without asking what it was. No going back now. "I'm going to have to work this around my schedule at the Farm & Home, you know."

"Oh, sure. No timetable on any of this. Let's go down and say hello to Max."

Max, the camp director, was in his thirties, slender and balding, with plaid shorts and a polo shirt that had some designer's name on it. They shook hands. "What's this I heard about a big bust over the river a while back?" he asked Grandpa. "Neo-Nazis across the bridge?"

Grandpa snorted. "Not hardly." He glanced at Mark. "We know the family. The only thing Charley Blankenship believes in is more money for Charley Blankenship. I've had to chase him away from here a couple of times."

"You have?" Mark said.

"Yep. Never mentioned it because I know you're friends with the boy, and I didn't want to color your opinion. Didn't seem right. Nothing ever turned up missing."

"Well, that's good, I guess." Grandpa's definitions of right and wrong were clear to himself at least, although Mark couldn't always discern them.

A few more friendly words, and all was settled. Mark would come by on his off days to pitch in, keeping his own timecard, for ten dollars an hour in cash. They shook on the deal; "That's the way we handle it out here in the country, right?" Max said, pleased with himself. And Mark began his second career as a part-time caretaker at the Nature Camp, his grandpa's assistant.

It was a pleasant enough life, customer service at the Farm & Home, loading sacks of mulch into customers' cars and sweeping up spills. Soon enough he was running the register during some shifts, a sign of growing trust. He kept his room in the basement of his parents' house, and every week he put a hundred dollars on the kitchen counter for groceries and rent, although his parents never asked for it; the action just seemed proper somehow. There was a girl named Missy, from Marquand, just a year older, who worked at the Farm & Home. She was friendly and encouraging, though a little shy, which suited Mark fine. He had never been confident around girls. By the end of summer they were going out, and at her house in October, with her parents off to Cape Girardeau for a day at the mall, they had clumsy, careful sex in her bedroom, stuffed animals watching from a high shelf. It wasn't mad passion but it felt good, and afterward they lay together enjoying the novelty of being naked with another person.

The cash from the Nature Camp accumulated little by little, though it dwindled in the fall and winter as the operation closed down. But Mark still drove out to Grandpa's once a week, and they checked the empty compound for weather damage and animal incursions. With the horses gone, they could wander the empty barn, nested snugly into the hillside, with its six-inch timbers and a family of raccoons living in the loft. "This barn'll outlast my house if they can keep a good roof on it," Grandpa mused. This thought seemed to spark other thoughts, and as they rode the golf cart home, he asked Mark to stay a bit.

They sat on the couch and unwrapped their Jolly Ranchers. "I expect you have been hearing from everybody and his dog about what you should do next," Grandpa said. "Especially since I hear that you have a girlfriend now."

Mark shifted in his seat, uncomfortable with where this was heading. Grandpa was a godly man, and although not a preacher himself had raised one, so his thoughts on morality were clear. Mark and Missy had been finding private spots almost weekly these days, and Mark guessed that word was getting around.

But Grandpa's thoughts were tending in a different direction. "You don't remember your grandmother, but this was her dad's farm. He had bought it back in the days when you could actually make a living on a farm. His people were from Bollinger County, but he was one of five boys, so they had to find their own places. When he couldn't keep it up any longer, I took over. I thought maybe your daddy would take over from me someday, but he got the call, which is fine, and as a pastor he needs to live in town. A man has to do what's best for himself and his family."

They heard the sound of a truck passing on the county road, and both craned their necks to see who it was. McMillion from up Dry Creek.

Grandpa continued. "So when the time comes for me to move off the farm, I'll have some choices to make." He leaned forward and tapped the glass top of the coffee table as if laying out cards. "I could sell it locally, although I doubt if anybody local could meet my price. I could sell it out of local. This close to the river, somebody would probably want to make a resort out of it, or one of those bee-n-bees. Or I could let you live in it, rent free, or maybe just transfer you the deed so that the government couldn't come after it if I end up in the nursing home."

He stood up. "That's what I wanted to tell you. Think it over and talk with your folks. The point is, we are people with roots. You can't make a living farming on a patch of ground this size anymore, but it's a solid house with good water. Not everybody wants to live way out here in the woods, and I understand that. You have to get your internet off the dish, and people tell me it only works about half the time." He held the door open for Mark. "No rush. I don't plan to die anytime soon."

But of course there was a rush, one generation passeth and another generation cometh, time's winged chariot as Mr. Seltzer had told them in English class, reading a poem that he didn't go into very deeply because they all had figured out that it was really about sex. Just last week they had gone to the funeral of another one of Grandpa's buddies, who had gone to the doctor for a checkup and come out with a death sentence. And the others who had fallen off their tractors, or had the tractors fall on them, or who had gone foggy with the worst killer of all, the one they dreaded the most and hardly dared even to speak about.

Mark had never thought of himself as a person with roots. He was just a guy, as far as he had ever considered it, with the usual loyalties to family and school. *Roots* seemed more mysterious, something for people with family crests, and it made him think of the ladies from the Historical Society who always set up a booth at the county fair. But he liked the idea of a place of his own, a place to entertain friends, one that even had river frontage and its own modest landmark, a big flat rock that jutted out into the current. He had fished with Grandpa off that rock a hundred times as a kid, and used it as a landing for the john boat they gigged from in the wintertime.

For the rest of the winter he mused about it, and as he restocked shelves in the Farm & Home, he watched Missy from a distance, ringing up customers with a blank expression until someone she knew came through the line. Missy was all right. They had good times. But once he had a place of his own, the weight of it all would begin to gather. Missy had already made the old remark about getting the milk and buying the cow. The longer he hung around, the closer he came to the moment when continuing to hang around became his only option.

And then in the early spring Charley Blankenship wandered into the store. Charley Blankenship of all people, as if nothing had happened, thicker and darker than Mark remembered, with a gray cast to his complexion as if he had been stored underground somewhere, which Mark supposed was not far from true. Mark slipped behind the swinging doors to the back storage area. He didn't want to talk to Charley and actually felt a little afraid, for he was a man who had been to prison, and heaven only knows what he had been through. Mark watched through the window as Charley roamed the aisles. The manager tried to discreetly follow him around, clumsily obvious as he pushed the restocking cart from aisle to aisle. Charley took a deliberately roundabout path through the store, feigning interest in motor oil and humorous greeting cards before placing each item carefully back on the shelf.

The charade went on so long that Mark finally came out of the back room. "Hi, Mr. Blankenship," he said. "Anything I can help you with?"

"Well, looky there! You working here now?"

Apparently he wanted an accidental meeting, so Mark played along. "Yes, sir. Here since summer."

Charley gave off an aroma that Mark thought might be stale alcohol. "Big changes all the way around," he said. "John Wayne into the Army. You into the working world. And me——" He grinned. "I guess everybody remembers."

"Yes, sir. I guess so."

"You hear much out of John Wayne?"

"Not a whole lot, Mr. Blankenship. Facebook message now and then." Wayne Blankenship's Facebook posts were usually GIFs of people falling into swimming pools or running into electric fences, and Mark couldn't remember actually getting a message from him that wasn't likely a hacker's work, but he decided that the bare truth was unnecessary at this moment.

"Yeah, neither one of us is much to communicate. They didn't let us use computers in the pen, so I lost track. A letter once in a while." Charley straightened himself and looked around. "Well, I don't want to keep you. Just came in to browse." Then he seized him by the bicep with a painful grip. "Listen. I have a message I need to get to John Wayne. Can you help me?" He released his hold after an instant, but Mark got the point.

"Of course."

"Good. Come out to my place tonight. Eleven or later."

Then he was out the door, and Mark was left with the feeling that he had been maneuvered into something, but he didn't know what. Nothing to do but follow through.

He waited till eleven, then left his basement bedroom quietly. He went out through the garage to his truck, parked in the driveway, and drove out of town. In the night he watched for deer and possums, armadillos, raccoons.

Blankenship stood in his front yard, a beer in hand, as Mark pulled up. "Hi, Mr. Blankenship," Mark said, climbing out of his truck.

Charley made a world-encompassing gesture with his beer. He didn't move to go inside. "Take a look around. I'm clearing out tomorrow. The marshals are seizing the property and gave me a day to pack up my shit."

"Can they do that?"

Charley shrugged. "Asset forfeiture, name of the game these days. I kinda hate it, the property's been in my family a long time. But the house is getting pretty crappy. I expect they'll just doze it and auction the acreage."

There was a stock trailer hooked up to Charley's pickup, half-loaded with household goods. "I guess I'd better let you get back to it," Mark said. "What's the message for John Wayne?"

"Not so fast." Charley looked him over. "This is a delicate situation."

He set the beer on the fender of the trailer and walked closer. "It's not so much a message as a thing. Let's drive and I'll explain on the way." He climbed into the passenger side of Mark's truck and waved him in.

Mark's stomach sank as he picked his way down Blankenship's lane to the county road. Charley sat in silence until they reached the junction. "Left," he said. "Cross the bridge and then stop."

The trip to the bridge took only a minute, but to Mark it felt like an hour, as Charley remained silent. What had happened to him in prison? Mark didn't remember him as this abrupt, alarming figure, someone who exuded a veiled sense of menace by his simple presence. Or maybe it was all in his anxious mind. They reached the bridge, crossed it, and stopped.

"Now switch off your lights and creep along," Charley said. "When you get to the Nature Camp gate, turn in."

"Mr. Blankenship, I'm not so sure about this," Mark said, his voice wobbly. "These are good people I deal with."

"Relax, I ain't gonna take anything. I'm on parole, son."

"Grandpa says he used to have to run you off from there."

Charley snorted. "Maybe twice out of the thirty or forty times I've been in there. But I never took a thing from them. Never took so much as a pool noodle, even though they left them laying around all the time. Don't shit in your own nest, that the thief's first rule."

By now they had reached the entry gate. Mark stopped his truck.

"Drive down as close as you can to the archery range without leaving tracks," Charley said. Mark couldn't think of anything to do except what he was told. He climbed out, unlocked the gate, and drove through.

It was a warm enough night for peep frogs but cool enough to feel a shiver as they stepped out at the archery range. When they reached the end of the path, Charley took a small black flashlight out of his back pocket and switched it on. They walked around the shooting stand to the straw bales stacked at the edge of the woods, where the instructors mounted targets in the summer. Charley aimed the beam of light at the base of the leftmost stack of bales.

"Here's my message for John Wayne," he said. "Over the years I've been setting a little bit aside all the time, for when he maybe got married or wanted to buy a house or some shit. It's in a two-pound Folgers can, one of those plastic ones, with duct tape around the lid. But now they're going to be watching my bank account, and every other damn thing about me. Can't even send him a gift card at Christmas time. Come tomorrow, I'll be out of here with a new name and that's the last anybody will ever hear of me." He paused. "So if he ever comes back, walk him out here and show him the spot. What he does after that is up to him. Take it, leave it, call the sheriff."

Charley walked back to the truck.

"Don't you want to check on it?" Mark asked.

He shrugged. "I know what's there, and you don't need to know."

As he turned the truck around and inched toward the entrance, driving more by memory than by sight, Mark realized why Charley had gotten out of prison so fast. He had turned informer, and now his life was not his own. Tomorrow he would become someone else, in a strange place, cut off forever from what he was before. Charley Blankenship wasn't much of a figure around here, but at least he was Charley Blankenship.

"But why'd you pick me?" Mark said.

"You're the only friend of his as I know of. I'm sure he's got other friends, but you're the only one I know." Charley got out to close the gate. "And besides, you're his teammate. That counts for something. Salt 'n' Pepa, right? And you'll likely be around here when he gets out of the service, if they don't blow him up over in Afghanistan or wherever. You're from around here."

Mark stepped out of the truck to make sure the lock was firmly closed, and as he did the two of them were transfixed by a beam of light from across the highway, which held steady on them for several seconds. They stared into it like the possums that Mark had dodged on his way out, glassy-eyed and captured. Then Charley said, "Hey, Ott," and the beam of light lowered. It was Grandpa in his golf cart, his gig light plugged into the outlet, an incredulous look on his face.

There they stood. Mark felt as though he was about to lose his balance, as if a sinkhole was opening under his feet between him and Grandpa. Then Grandpa broke the silence. "Well, I never," he said. He switched off his light and drove home.

The darkness surrounded Mark, and his ears buzzed. Charley cleared his throat. "If you need to go explain to your grandpa what you were doing here, go ahead. And he'll have a deputy here in the morning with a search warrant and a backhoe. And I'll be upset, and maybe headed back to the can, but maybe not. I can't do nothing about it. I can't threaten you, so I won't even try." He turned away. "You go on, I'll walk home."

He disappeared into the starlit night. Mark remained in the driveway of the Nature Camp a while longer, trying to figure things out. He owed nothing to Charley Blankenship by any human measure, nor to Wayne for that matter, whom he wouldn't have called "friend" had Charley not used the word. Yet he felt as though an obligation had been laid on him anyway, without his asking for it, and he didn't know how to discharge it. Grandpa would want to know what he had been doing out there, and he deserved an answer.

But Mark wasn't quite ready to give it. If all this talk of roots meant anything, surely it included Grandpa giving him a little grace time, the bit of space he needed to work his way through the layers of duty that rested on him. He climbed in his truck and headed toward town.

Grandpa's house was dark, but Mark knew he was watching. He was probably sitting on the porch right now, wondering about him, and Mark could only hope that he would grant him that grace, listen to his explanation, and trust him if he decided to keep Charley

Blankenship's secret. Keep it, don't keep it: neither felt right. He flashed his headlights as he passed the house, a salute, a signal, a plea, although at the moment he had neither the words to express what he wanted to say nor the thoughts he wanted to express.

As he topped the final ridge before town, its scattered lights lay before him, like someone's Christmas decorations tossed in the yard, still lit. He slowed to a stop and took them all in. House lights, streetlights, business lights, all spread out in the valley, seemingly random but somehow connected, if only he could see the pattern.

Somewhere in that tangle was the light in front of his parents' house, and the lights that patterned the parking lots around his dad's church, and the hissing yellow sodium-vapor lights that surrounded the Farm & Home. Everything serenely illuminated, the darkness held at bay. Mark would have liked for one of those lights to be his, and his alone. But for now he would have to navigate from borrowed light to borrowed light as best he could.

He put the truck in drive and headed down the hill, for it was going to be an early day tomorrow.

Why Miss Elizabeth Never Joined the Shakespeare Club

They found Miss Elizabeth dead this morning, upright in her velvet Queen Anne chair, hands folded. When I heard the news, I was in the same pose; I had fallen asleep while crocheting, as I am prone to do in the afternoons nowadays, and the telephone frightened me. Unexpected phone calls always bring thoughts of death. My first reaction: *Now I am the only one left who knows Miss Elizabeth's story.* My second reaction: *Perhaps I am the only one to whom it has meaning.*

Miss Elizabeth's story involves the Shakespeare Club. Founded sometime during Piedmont's early, dirty, railhead years, the club has remained the town's pinnacle of acceptance ever since. A lady cannot join until the age of fifty; sixty is more usual. Once a month, the club meets in a member's home to scrutinize the host's silver patterns and to decide whom to exclude. As far as I know, Shakespeare himself is mentioned only at the April meeting, when the ladies wreathe garlands in their thin gray hair and recite passages to celebrate his birthday.

Miss Elizabeth was a Peck, of the savings-and-loan Pecks; an Episcopalian by birth; and, though not a widow, was the next best thing—an old maid. In other words, an ideal Shakespeare clubber. That she had never been accepted into this select circle puzzled Piedmont continually; and it was the club, not the pariah, that suffered in the community's esteem.

Some attributed it to the innocent fact that Miss Elizabeth and Mrs. Harvel Dodson, past president, were bitter enemies. This explanation points to the early days, when, in the years before he founded the lumbermill that still bears his name, Mr. Harvel Dodson chased Miss Elizabeth like a pup; until one night at a dance, while Mr. Harvel was waltzing with his eventual wife (then merely Vera Beck, a solemn, wide-hipped farm girl from Beckville), Miss Elizabeth made one of her famous sharp remarks, a quip about Miss Vera's broad pastures, in front of a chuckling group. There ensued a quarrel, which the bright-eyed Elizabeth won swiftly and mercilessly. But, this theory holds, the ugly incident drove Mr. Harvel out of Miss Elizabeth's orbit and into that of Miss Vera, and drove a barb of enmity into Miss Vera's heart that only exclusion from the Shakespeare Club could salve, long after the decease of their quarrel's immediate source (for Mr. Harvel died under a stray load of logs scarcely seven years later).

But this is not it. The Shakespeare Club has been a fertile home for hatreds ever since its inception. Indeed, enemies make the best prospects for new members; for then, not only does the enemy owe her rival an unrepayable favor—nomination to the exclusive circle— but she must also endure the sniffing at her wall decorations and smirking at her book collection of a dozen of the town's finest ladies. A good example from Miss Elizabeth's time is Miss Louise Wasson, town gossip, whose car appeared on the scene of every violent death or mayhem in western Wayne County. Miss Louise was invited to join only so the club members could be sure she wasn't gossiping about *them* one afternoon a month.

Miss Elizabeth taught piano; and, once a week from the time I was six until my twelfth birthday, my mother curried me down, pulled a dress from the best-clothes section of my closet, and sent me off for an hour of finger-stretching in Miss Elizabeth's back parlor. My chubby fingers strained to make the reach from C to A as Miss Elizabeth perched over me, singing the insipid lyrics from *Teaching Little Fingers to Play* that sought to give those mindless exercises some sense: Now-my-scale-is-going-way-up! Now-my-scale-is-going-back-*down*. Now-it's-up! Now-it's-*down*. The afternoon that I'm remembering now, the afternoon when Miss Elizabeth permanently forewent her rightful spot in the Shakespeare Club, occurred about midway in my career as a piano pupil. I was ten; Miss Elizabeth, at least fifty by then. It was late August. Leaves drooped, deep green and waxy, on the water oaks that lined Peck Lane; gnats clouded the air outside her parlor windows. My starched dress chafed the backs of my thighs.

In the years that had passed since their original falling-out, Miss Elizabeth, the slender coquette, slowly vitrified and shrank, growing brittle and more blue-veined, while Mrs. Harvel Dodson's youthful solemnity sank into humorlessness, and her wide hips, as prophesied, became wide everything. Only a few years older than her rival but already a twenty-five-year widow, Mrs. Dodson was precocious in the Shakespeare Club; they invited her to join in her first year of eligibility and accepted her into the club on the first ballot. Already she had perfected the air of invulnerable Pharisaical piety that most club members fail to attain until their seventies; and recognizing her advancement, the Shakespeares elected her president in only her third year—the year that Miss Elizabeth was blackballed on her first two acceptance votes.

Mrs. Dodson, as I have said, was a farm girl, who occasionally horrified her social circle by remarking that she had personally wrung the necks of chickens or participated in the castration of hogs. That all ended when she married and moved to town, of course, but after Mr. Dodson's hasty departure she renewed one link to her past by renting a garden plot at the deserted Benton place, at the end of Benton Lane. In March, she would send old Bill Ruengert out there with his mule to plow up a patch of ground, and during the spring and early summer, Mrs. Dodson could be seen walking briskly down Benton Lane, wearing a faded navy-blue pinafore and an old straw bonnet that would have been more suited to Ruengert's mule.

Miss Elizabeth's house stood at the end of Peck Lane, across a deep wooded ravine from the old Benton place. We town kids had attempted to explore the ravine, a tangle of saw briers and poison ivy, bindweed and buckbrush, without success; no paths entered it from any direction. But from Miss Elizabeth's back parlor (Now-my-scale-is-going-way-up!) I could watch Mrs. Harvel Dodson's stocky blue figure wink in and out, like the moon among clouds, behind bushes and light poles and tree trunks until she reached the brown square plot at Benton's. With my young eyes, I could see her clearly. Miss Elizabeth used binoculars.

Once at her plot, Mrs. Harvel Dodson would dig and spade and hoe, "like a field hand," Miss Elizabeth once murmured, lowering her binoculars, as I shifted on the unkind padding of her piano bench. At intervals she would plop on the grass, legs splayed, resting against a tree and fanning herself with that ratty straw bonnet. Miss Elizabeth would cluck softly and return to my lessons with "Very good, dear. Now try Number 28. Stop crossing your fingers!" and then ease back to the window, binoculars in hand.

That afternoon, Miss Elizabeth suddenly drew in her breath, like someone sucking a sore tooth. I knew something was up, but had the presence of mind to keep playing my scales as I shifted around for a better look, hating starch and its tell-tale rustle. But I needn't have worried, for Miss Elizabeth, engrossed in new visions, was snapping her binoculars about like a tank commander. My fingers automatically continued their run (Now-it's-up! Now-it's-*down*) as I peered over my shoulder to the old Benton place, where Mrs. Harvel Dodson had laid down her grubhoe and entered the decaying house through a back door I had always supposed was locked.

We children knew that the Benton place was haunted, even though we weren't allowed any closer than McGinley's, the next-to-last house, a good seventy yards up the lane. "An old rat-trap," the grownups called it, having mistaken the gibberings of its trapped souls for mere rodent squeaks. My astonishment at seeing Mrs. Dodson brave the house's interior broke my hand's autonomous progress for a moment (now-it's!), but Miss Elizabeth didn't notice. She had trained her scrutiny out into waste fields behind the old mansion, once Mr. Emory Benton's prize pastureland and private golf course, now overgrown with sage grass and cedar sprouts, where the figure of a man—as it approached, we saw it to be Mr. Miller Weems, the Ford dealer, a married man—picked its way around the clumps of sassafras and persimmon, treading gingerly over the rabbit warrens and mounds of grass, invisible from the other houses on Benton Lane, invisible from all vantages, in fact, except Miss Elizabeth's back parlor. He stopped at the back-yard gate and attempted for a moment to undo its rust-caked latch, then stepped through the fallen fence, brushing off his hands, leaving the gate to stand forever closed. He walked without hesitation to the back door and stepped inside without knocking.

Which brings me to the Dog Lady. The Dog Lady, whose real name was Fannie, lived down in the creek bottoms with a pack of about twenty starving curs and an occasional man. We girls were forbidden to explore the narrow dirt path that led to her shack, although the boys bragged that they had gotten close enough to hit it with rocks, which always produced a rush of dogs and a sputter of curses from within. About once a month, the Dog Lady and her entourage came into the main part of town, and our mothers called us inside as they passed; actually, we had less to fear than our pets did, for though the dogs would merely sniff our legs and trot on, they would set on any yard dog that challenged them, and if they isolated one away from its house, they would ring around it and tear it to shreds. In April we would see them foraging in the woods around Clark's Mountain as the Dog Lady searched for mushrooms and yarbs; in June we would swerve by them in our car, my father clenching his teeth and swearing, as she hunted the ditches for empty bottles; in August she systematically worked the trash cans of Piedmont, throwing choice items into a burlap sack. And on that August day of my childhood, as I struggled with sharps and flats in

Miss Elizabeth's talcum-scented air, the Dog Lady came down Benton Lane, rummaging in garbage barrels and kicking at indefinable objects flattened in the street.

Miss Elizabeth stood stiff at the window. I could have sworn she was quivering, like a pointer hound that has spotted a pheasant. There, humping and hobbling up the lane, came the bewhiskered old woman. Her dogs trotted beside her, coming near and then circling out in eccentric orbits like straying comets. She squatted behind a bush and relieved herself, then began to dig in the piles of junk and dead grass that had accumulated in the yard.

By now I had stopped playing my exercise entirely. Miss Elizabeth did not turn around and look at me; she was talking softly to herself, clutching the binoculars, and (now I am sure) quivering. I tiptoed up beside her; she gave no notice.

Suddenly one of the dogs, a lank, yellow-spotted hound, darted toward the house and captured some small animal near the front steps; he worried it with his teeth as he held it under tight-set front paws. At first I thought that it was a rat, but when the Dog Lady wobbled over with her sack and tried to snatch it away from the dog, I decided it had to be a rabbit. The two of them fought a brief tug-of-war with it for a moment—by now, the rest of the pack was gathering curiously around, sniffing in and jumping back—until Fannie yanked the rabbit away and retreated through the mass of excited dogs. The yellow hound pursued. He leaped repeatedly after his prize as the Dog Lady backed away, each leap ending in a snapping narrow miss. Finally, Fannie's arm tired, or perhaps the dog gathered up some hidden strength; for in a twisting leap he seized the rabbit and, judging by her sudden stagger, part of the Dog Lady's hand as well.

Instantly, the whole pack dived for the treasure. We saw the Dog Lady falter, buffeted by the frenzied dogs, then give a convulsive yank back, like a rearing horse, holding firm to the embattled rabbit. As she sought to lift her prize above her head—still fumbling with the sack in her other hand—she pulled four dogs off the ground, two gripping the rabbit and two her forearm. One dog came away with a mouthful of cloth from her sleeve; others dug at her legs and ankles.

The battle continued from the front yard down to the garden plot, back into the side yard, and finally up against the house, where Fannie was able to brace herself against the wall and kick at her treasonous crew. The yellow dog still clung to her arm; she knocked it off against a porch post. We watched through a screen of parlor palms as Fannie, kicking and batting at the dogs, the rabbit held high above her head, crept edgewise along the wall of the house until lurching into—and then through—the unlocked back door, with the scrambling pack close behind.

Miss Elizabeth held the binoculars to her eyes just long enough to see two figures, the woman in pink underwear and the man clutching a half-raised pair of pants around his knees, stumble out the front door. They hesitated. The woman plunged into the jungly ravine separating the two houses; the man hop-dashed for the back fields like a sack race contestant. She lowered her spyglasses and, turning, noticed me for the first time. "My, my," was all she said. Then she walked past me to the telephone and made two calls. The first (and out of respect for the dead I attribute her motive to charity) was to the city marshal, Jug Wilson: "Please hurry," she said, "there's been a terrible accident at the end of Benton Lane," and hung up. The second was to Miss Louise Wasson, town gossip: "Loozy dear," she said, "what on *earth* is going on down at the old Benton place?" There was a moment for Miss Louise's reply; then she said, "Why, the police car and the ambulance just went roaring past, and they went down the old Benton lane, and I thought something *awful* must have happened . . . Well, I thought you might know. Bye, dear."

Miss Elizabeth walked back to the window, saying to me as she passed, "Now, let's go through each one once more, and try for no mistakes." Obediently, I sat down and played scales until my time was up. Miss Elizabeth gazed into the ravine all the while; soon, the police car and ambulance went by, sirens screaming, followed closely by the Wasson Buick. The ambulance took the Dog Lady off within minutes. Jug Wilson stayed on well past dusk—having shut the dogs inside the house, he lured them out one by one, shot each dog, cut off its head and put it in a bag for the rabies tests, and buried the bodies in the back yard. Miss Louise stayed for it all.

During the hours that Mrs. Harvel Dodson crouched in that ravine, waving away mosquitoes, imagining copperheads, trying to remember what poison ivy looked like, she no doubt had time to think—to envision Miss Louise poking through the house and finding her clothes (luckily for her, Miss Louise stayed in her car, and Jug figured the mattress and clothes belonged to some kids); to consider the astonishingly quick arrival of the marshal, ambulance, and town gossip; to calculate vantages, with her eye ending up at Miss Elizabeth's back parlor where it peeked out through a gap in the surrounding shrubbery; in other words, to put two and two together, to count trumps and come up one short.

So it happened—or more accurately, so it hung. The story was never told. It *couldn't* be told, really. For this was a genuine secret, not one of the idle, fine-spun fictions that Piedmont relishes so greatly. It was the real thing, the kind that wrecks lives, and its release could have set off an unraveling of the social fabric far beyond its immediate target, the way the loose thread you pluck at in the hem of your dress suddenly ladders up under your tug and pulls the whole garment apart. Miss Elizabeth knew that; I knew that.

Mrs. Harvel Dodson's reputation remained unblemished. But having infinitely more to lose from any exchange of innuendo with Miss Elizabeth, Vera Dodson not only blackballed her from the club a third time, but gave up her garden plot and avoided her for the rest of her life. She grew broader and grimmer as the decades passed and developed strange habits, grinding her teeth loudly and speaking to invisible companions. She died, grim-faced, a dozen years ago.

As for myself, I learned chords and simple accompaniment, and then quit. Nothing compelling ever arose to draw me from Piedmont, so I stayed, married, raised a family. I am a widow myself now, and in a few more years, perhaps the Shakespeare Club will invite my application. The club is having difficulty attracting new members; it's too stodgy for today's active senior citizens, who attend the Wednesday lunches at the Retired Persons' Center and vie for seats in the Silver Haired Legislature.

I continued to visit Miss Elizabeth; she would receive me in her front parlor, as desiccated and fragile in her velvet Queen Anne chair as a butterfly on a pin. We never spoke of that day; and if I blundered, if the conversation edged out toward that ravine, her bright, tiny eyes would lance me through the still air, jolting me back to my childhood timidity, an unguarded phrase left dangling from my lips.

But this morning the mailman found her dead in that chair in a pose of rapt attention, her hands folded politely, her glittering eyes wide. And with her death our town has finally crossed the line into the modern age, our draggletailed, loquacious age, where no thought need be kept secret and any deed is acceptable so long as it's sincere. Miss Elizabeth left the world this morning; the world had left her long before.

Fannie has outlived them all. She lost an arm to infection, but as a result won a substantial increase in her welfare payments, which she used to rent a house nearer town; in April I see her trudging toward the woods, her sack in her hand, a new pack of dogs beside her. The houses—the Benton place now completely collapsed, the Peck place deserted (perhaps haunted) and destined for the same eventual fate—still squat back to back across the ravine from each other, like a grumpy couple exchanging silences.

Trio Sonata in C

APRIL, six in the morning, and Tom hears Grandpa doing his morning check of the downstairs doors and windows. One by one they rattle—kitchen, dining room, nook, living room, hallway, back storage, utility room. He looks over. Elizabeth is still asleep. So is his left arm, pinned underneath her, and he remembers that they had made love sometime after midnight, when he got in from Atlanta, and had fallen asleep still entangled. He eases the arm out and sits up, feeling a blot of pain roll down his artery like a ball bearing. She doesn't stir. Tom slides out of bed and finds his robe, pads downstairs avoiding the third step from the top, which squeaks.

Grandpa is at the kitchen table now, his .22 pistol beside his plate. He has emptied a jar of maraschino cherries into a white cereal bowl and scoops them out one at a time: slurps the sugar water from his spoon, contemplates the glowing half-cherry for a moment, then picks it off with the tip of his tongue. He has switched to his summer outfit of overalls and flannel shirt. He does not look up.

"Good morning, Thomas," Grandpa says, his gaze fixed on the last cherry dipping and weaving at the bottom of the bowl. "You're up early today."

"You want an egg?"

"If I had wanted an egg, I would have gotten an egg," Grandpa says. The last cherry disappears into his snapping toothless jaws. A moment of gumming, and then he lifts the bowl to his extended lips, draining the thick pink juice in one noisy gulp.

"Wish you wouldn't carry that gun in the house."

"No point in checking for robbers if you don't have a gun."

He sets the bowl down reverently and moves to the window, his steps firm but slow. A few seconds later, the tip of the sun breaks the horizon of housetops out the kitchen window, and he jots in a notebook pulled from his overall pocket: sunrise 6:04, 51 degrees.

Tom heads back upstairs and slips into his side of the bed. Elizabeth is awake.

"Is it Dad?"

"Yes, don't worry. He's having breakfast."

Tom hears the steps descending into the basement, which has become entirely Grandpa's domain since he moved in three years ago. He thinks: today is Thursday. *Trio Sonata in C.* As soon as he thinks it, the opening organ chords ease up through the floorboards. The bass tones buzz angrily out of the cheap, tinny speakers of Grandpa's stereo, a gift from Elizabeth's damfool brother Willie, who only has to put up with it at Christmas and for three weeks in the summer. It used to be Bach's Trio Sonata every morning, until Elizabeth gave him *Living Guitars Play Lennon/McCartney,* which now gets Monday, Wednesday, and Friday. The rest of the stack—twenty or thirty CDs by now—is never played.

Her arm slides over his chest.

"Go back to sleep, honey," she says. "You still have forty-five minutes."

"Okay."

SEPTEMBER, Tom loads the fireplace for the first time this season, hickory logs from Willie's lake property. Grandpa scoots his chair close, propping his feet on the extra logs lying on the fireplace apron, while Jeff and Tommy Junior click their PlayStations on the couch.

"Good wood, hickory," Grandpa says. "Burns clean."

Everyone knows he's not speaking to anyone in particular, so no one answers.

"Me and Pa had a job cutting one year," he says. "That was for this old Bohunk at the Mine la Motte railyard. Wanted to pay me half wages, but Pa says no. 'Enos does the work of a man, he gets the wage of a man,' Pa told him. Damn near had it out with that old bastard before all was said and done, too."

Tom and Elizabeth pass a glance. He's tried to persuade her to talk to the old man about his language, have him clean it up around the kids, but she resists: he's just an old dirt farmer, she pleads, too old to change.

The evening goes on, quiet and ordinary; the kids play, Tom and Elizabeth read, Grandpa tells old stories to himself. Flipping through the financial pages, Tom realizes with surprise that he has been grinding his teeth all evening, that his shoulders are knotty and tense. This is the ideal he has pictured—the handsome wife, the bright, well-behaved kids, the good job, the two-story house. But that dotty old creature in front of the fireplace blemishes his picture. He closes his eyes.

"What's your schedule this week?" Elizabeth murmurs in a what-are-you-thinking-about voice.

"Home-based until Wednesday, then I have to fly a bunch of them to the new plant site in Minnesota. We'll stay one night and be back Thursday."

He tries to find his place on the page again. Grandpa starts a new story, one that he thinks is funny; he laughs and slaps his chair arms noiselessly. He scoots closer to the fire, but it doesn't seem to warm him, for he pulls his sweater tighter. A few minutes later, he gives up.

"Guess I'll plug in the old blanket."

At this Grandpa laughs again, high and creaky like the squealing of hand brakes on a boxcar and goes downstairs to his room.

"Hot in here," says Tom, and steps into the backyard. Elizabeth follows him.

"Something the matter?"

"No, nothing. Just hot."

He picks up a few fallen twigs, noticing that the lawn, which at first glance is a uniform green carpet, reveals more and more imperfections the longer he looks. Here a scalped spot, here a shaggy patch where the grass lay wet and flat escaping last week's mowing, here a clump of chickweed and henbit where the Kentucky blue didn't take. He thinks of flying, and how at a certain altitude and airspeed—very low and very fast—the whole earth is a lawn, green and even, silent, perfect.

It's his favorite sensation, that feeling of hurtling, transcendent, past trivialities and flaws; it reminds him of his teenage years, when he and Elizabeth were going steady. Every summer he came down from the city to visit his uncle's farm, and she was the neighbor girl. Ripping down the farm-to-market roads in his car, a '65 Mustang he had restored—one hand on hers, the other on the steering wheel—he'd glance to the side and see the weeds and flowers and rocks all blend into a rush of brown and green. He was clear, she was clear, and the rest of the world was an unimportant blur.

"Watch for thunderstorms this trip," she says, startling him. "Seems like there's always storms this time of year."

"Don't worry, I'm hauling board members, so we'll take the jet instead of the twin-engine. We'll skip around the storms like they're standing still."

OCTOBER, bedtime, the kids troop into the study for their kiss. Tommy Junior hangs behind for a moment, an intent expression—it's almost a pout—crossing his face.

"Dad, what's the cut that never heals?"

Tom turns away to set his book down, thinking and pursing his lips, then turns back to lay his hand softly on Tommy's shoulder. The contrast makes his hand look larger than it really is and makes Tommy's shoulder look smaller than it really is, and he has to smile at that for a moment, the sight of his hand covering that tiny innocent neck, a truly fatherly gesture, he thinks. By now they both know that the rest of the conversation is a formality, that Tommy's asked about a bad word and isn't going to learn anything more here, and Tom says: "Where'd you pick up that phrase?"

"Grandpa taught us a song, a song about a cut that never heals, but feels better when you rub it."

"Well, he's your grandpa, so you have to listen when he talks. But what he told you wasn't nice, because it says bad things about girls. So you go on and get your bath and get ready for bed, and don't sing that song again. It's not polite. Go on now."

Tom knows he'll be singing it on the playground tomorrow, pretending to know what it means, but he tries to suppress that thought as Tommy dashes away. The boys race to the bathroom; Elizabeth follows to supervise. She stops in the doorway.

"Something new?"

"Dirty songs. I guess I'll talk to him."

"I can try."

"You talk to him in the morning. I'll see what I can do tonight."

He flips on the stairway light and calls into the dark: "You still awake down here?"

Grandpa is covered to the chin with a heavy comforter. He switches on the bedside lamp, revealing a ragged thermal under-wear cuff, then pulls his hand back under the covers. An electric cord disappears into the quilted layers.

"You're teaching those kids things I don't want them to learn," Tom says. "At least not yet."

"I like to talk about old times," Grandpa says.

"Old times I don't mind. Sex I mind."

Grandpa seems to sink lower into the covers. His fingers hook over the edge of the quilt, and Tom thinks of chicken feet. He realizes he hasn't seen a live chicken in years, since—when? Since he came back from overseas, he guesses. Grandpa hunches his shoulders.

"What do you think they talk about on the playground? When I was their age, I was working every day, five or six hours after school. I'd come home after school . . . "

"You're not their age now. And you're not their father."

He knows Elizabeth is somewhere above him now, telling stories, tucking covers underneath chins, preserving order. He imagines her as a child, her father parting her thin blonde hair for a goodnight kiss on her forehead; his hands on her brow must have been smooth and hard, like polished oak.

"I can talk to my own grandkids. Somebody's got to tell them things. Since you're always flying off someplace. Better than picking it up on the playground."

Tom sits on the edge of the bed, one hand on the table and one on the thick pile of covers. He feels the rising warmth from the buried blanket.

"I'm always flying around. Okay. But I still don't need your help raising my kids."

In bed upstairs, Tom looks at the ceiling.

"Your father's not senile, not by a long shot," he says.

"No," Elizabeth says. "He can be very clear on things when he wants to."

"He's always very clear on things."

Elizabeth is quiet for a while. Then:

"It's hard for me to think of putting him in a home."

"He's already in a home."

CHRISTMAS approaches, Tom brings a sweater from California for Elizabeth's early present.

"Do you think Dad might have had a small stroke?" she asks in bed that night. "He has a hard time getting up the stairs anymore. He forgot Tommy's name today."

Tom rolls against her, thinking he ought to feel more tired than he does. He's been out of town for four days, first to that damn new plant in Minnesota, then to the regional office, and he had dangled her image in front of his mind all the way—just like this, alone, in bed, late. But she's not getting interested, she's busy thinking her thoughts.

"I don't know," he says. "What do you think?"

"I can't tell. He *is* getting old."

"Yes." Tom rolls onto his back and shuts his eyes; he doesn't want to hear about the old man. He lets his hand slide up Elizabeth's leg, over her breast, under her head. He massages her far shoulder. After a minute, he says:

"Do you think there's anything we should do?"

She curls toward his side, her nose rubbing in under his arm. A strand of her hair catches between them, and he shifts to free it.

"I don't know. Keep a close eye, I guess."

The streetlight casts a mercury-vapor glow through their window; it slants across the foot of the bed, a lumpy green rectangle, folds of cloth fenced by darkness. It reminds him of distant, forested hills. He imagines farms and villages in those hills, small farms with terraced fields and a few cattle, narrow lanes leading through tall grass to the village. Elizabeth squirms and shifts her leg; Tom smiles. Earthquake. He drifts toward sleep, dreams of descending out of the clouds and flying low and fast over green folded hills.

Living Guitars Play Lennon / McCartney comes on full blast at five-thirty. Elizabeth gets up at six to make biscuits, and Tom drags himself out, even though his body, still half in California, is saying three-thirty. At breakfast, Grandpa supports himself on the counter and chairs as he comes through the kitchen. Tom can't remember if this is new or if he's always leaned on things as he walks, but eventually decides it must be new. Grandpa eats as heartily as ever and calls everyone by their right names.

* * *

APRIL again, spring comes late. Elizabeth takes Jeff for an after-noon at the zoo. Tom uses the quiet time to gather up receipts and invoices for the tax return.

He starts with the doctor bills, which will be up from last year's, what with one broken arm and two new pairs of glasses. After a while, he hears the back door open and hears Grandpa's voice move into the living room. The recliner groans back, one notch, two notches.

"You bet I was in a war. What there was of it for me. I hardly got over there when it got called off."

Tommy's voice floats up: "Did you fight like Daddy did?"

"No, your daddy was a flier, and I was a ground man. We had to walk everywhere we went. But I imagine he killed plenty more of his enemy than I ever even saw."

"Did you fight a lot?"

"Mostly among ourselves. I remember I got into a fight with a nigger sergeant from our quartermaster outfit. They brought in a load of chocolate special from the States. 'Give me another one,' I said, 'I've always had a sweet tooth.' 'Everybody has a sweet tooth,' he said. 'Why, you God damn nigger,' I said, and I took a big ladle out of the soup pot and cracked him one across the nose. You can bet I got my extra chocolate from the boy that took his place. I've always had . . . "

There is a pause, and Tom stops adding the bills on the cal-culator. The pause lengthens into silence; the recliner moves up a notch. Footsteps across the floor, then:

"Grandpa?" More silence. Tom gets up. Then:

"What is it, boy?"

"You were talking about the fight."

"Oh yeah. I was pretty scrappy in my day."

MOTHER'S DAY he gives her a porcelain pitcher he saw in a Toronto antique shop.

"I'll be in Minnesota all next week. There's some kind of dispute."

The kids and Grandpa have been in bed for hours by now; when he came in, she was at the kitchen table, reading, because the chairs in the kitchen were the most comfortable, she said. The light from the kitchen, cold and blue, had carved out the corner of a desk, the back of a chair, a patch of the living room floor, as he walked through the darkened house with the fragile pitcher hidden behind his back.

She rises from her chair and fills a water glass from the tap.

"I hate to see you gone this much with Dad the way he is."

"Has something happened?"

"Nothing, really. Little things." She drinks a sip and pours the rest in the sink. Tom becomes aware of a cricket that must have been chirping, unnoticed, all this time. She says:

"The other night I heard him talking downstairs, as if Mama was there with him."

Although she doesn't move and continues to stand at the sink with her back to him, Tom can tell that she is crying now. Finally, she gives up and acknowledges it, wipes her cheek with the back of her hand, leaning down over the sink. But her voice, when she speaks again, is as controlled as before:

"When I was little I could hear them in the living room after I had gone to bed. They'd talk quietly, I never could make out words, just the sound of their voices. It made me feel good to know they were out there, and I was safe. That's the voice I heard downstairs."

She has stopped crying and sits back at the table, tucks a velvet bookmark into her novel. But she can't stay still; she gets up again and clears a place in the hutch for the pitcher.

"Willie went off to school just a few months after she died. I was only six then, and I used to wish for the sound of those voices again, and I'd call out. He'd sit on the edge of my bed and say, 'It's all right, baby girl,' and he'd pat my head."

She sits back at the table, across from him. The cricket stops, and the stillness that its cessation leaves seems to bring into being other, farther noises: some kid's loud muffler a block or two away, a train passing through the suburbs on its way to Union Station, downtown. She looks up at him hard.

"Can you understand?"

He doesn't know what to say, of course he understands, but he can't get out of the Minnesota trip now, it wasn't his idea to build a plant in Minnesota. But he realizes that her face is drawn, her eyes are red, so he squeezes her limp hand across the cold granite of the kitchen counter and says:

"Yes, I think so."

"Then do something. I'm sick with worry."

She pushes the chair back wearily and heads upstairs to bed. He turns out the light, feeling his eyes adjust to the sudden darkness. Perhaps I should take him out more, he thinks, get him some fresh air, but as soon as he thinks it, he realizes the poverty of the idea. A sense of his own inadequacy rises up before him, ugly and simple. He closes his eyes and tries to bring back even fields and the tops of clouds; tries for the ghostly, cool scene of a carrier at night, dropping in from two thousand feet. But the images won't come, and all he is left with are the slowly expanding magenta spheres inside his eyes.

MIDSUMMER, ten o'clock, and a power failure hits town. The kids groan when their TV show shrinks to a vanishing blip, but soon get caught up in the novelty of it, lighting candles and peering into the black streets. The transistor radio says it's most of the metro area, three million people or more; Grandpa sits in the recliner, his slippered feet level with his head.

"We used to have to stand guard duty in the war. You'd have a little house built up where you could see out over the cleared area.

'Course, you couldn't see anything, it was so dark, but you'd listen and hear things. Once in a while somebody'd shoot off a flare."

Jeff and Tommy Junior dart from window to window.

"Look," shouts Jeff, "you can't even see Mr. Dover's house."

"That's nothing," Tommy says. "I can't see the rosebushes. Look here."

"Me and Pa had a horse named Jack that was afraid of the dark," Grandpa says. "There was a covered bridge over the Musco that was on the road to Knob Lick, and Pa'd say 'Enos, don't you try to ride old Jack up thataway, or you'll get throwed for sure.'"

The lights stay off and soon the kids go to bed, Grandpa goes to bed. Tom and Elizabeth open their windows to the summer air and make love, slowly and easily.

At four in the morning, the sound of Grandpa's .22 cracks open the blacked-out stillness. A wooden chair—a dining room chair—falls over and clatters against the floor. Something breaks.

Tom flings out of bed in a single spasm, hitting the floor in a running crouch. His bearings are wrong, and he cracks his forehead against the corner of the dresser. Then he orients himself: window, window, door, and is out the door by the time Elizabeth has untangled herself from the hurled covers.

There's no sound from the children's rooms; he shuts their doors noiselessly and races down the stairs, skipping the third from the top. As he leaps into the kitchen on bare feet, he sees the newly risen moon through the nook window and thinks: you're showing a silhouette, get down, just as a second shot whines past him and shatters something in the cabinet above the sink.

Grandpa's voice calls out: "Who's there?" That fixes his location, at the end of the hallway a few feet from the basement door.

"Who's there?"

He circles through the kitchen and stops behind the dining room door.

He tries: "Grandpa?" The pistol cracks instantly and a bullet digs into the floor a few feet in front of him.

"Who is it? Who's there?"

"Grandpa, it's me."

This time the bullet hits the doorframe; splinters of wood sting his arms and stomach.

Tom circles back to the kitchen doorway, ducking to avoid the moonlit window. He's closer from this side, but the table and perhaps a chair are in the way. He hears the whirring of the battery-powered clock in the dining room, hears stirrings and footsteps upstairs, hears the motor of a car outside. A child's plaintive, questioning voice drifts down the stairwell, answered by Elizabeth's, low and melodic.

"Who's there?"

He tries to count shots but can't; remembers Grandpa's revolver has nine chambers. He closes his eyes and drops to one knee, his fingers tracing the faint patterns in the kitchen floor tile, and for a moment he rests with closed eyes, enjoying a field of vision unblemished by light or shadow. He tries:

"Enos?" No shot, no reply. He inhales slowly through his mouth. The child's voice drifts down again, sleepier, reassured. "Enos, boy? Is that you?"

He circles back to the other doorway now, listening with his skin and fingertips, listening with his nose and eyes: a footstep. Grandpa's voice, shaky and old, very old:

"Pa?"

Another footstep, and now it is Grandpa who is silhouetted in a window, his pistol half-lowered, his straining head fixed toward the kitchen door.

Tom comes in low and fast, very low and very fast, the carpet kissing the pads of his bare feet, the sound of his nerves stretching into a musical note higher than his ears can hear, and when he feels the carpet of the dining room end and the wood floor of the hallway begin he pulls up suddenly, seizing the old man around the hips, pinning his arms just below the elbows and lifting him off the floor. Grandpa's coarse underwear, fragrant with age and sweat, presses against Tom's face; his feet kick him harmlessly on the knees. Tom tightens his grip and shakes him, harder and harder; he lifts him higher into the air, squeezing until he hears the pistol clatter at his feet.

He has him now. But he doesn't know what to do with him. The old man's body is thin and light.

By now the coming dawn allows Tom to make out the details of the room a bit. He puts Grandpa down, loosening his grip slightly, feeling the tremble of his brittle arms. He looks to the window and sees their reflection—himself naked and hairy, Grandpa small in his grasp like a child. Grandpa puts his arms on Tom's shoulders.

"What is it, Thomas? What's the matter?"

"You're okay. It's morning. Breakfast isn't ready yet. Go back downstairs."

Grandpa turns toward his doorway, his hand reaching for support. "Okay. Breakfast." He stops on each step and looks around himself in wariness and wonder, as if stepping into a hall of mirrors or a no man's land. Tom watches him until he reaches the bottom step, then heads upstairs to find some clothes. A few minutes later, even though it's Friday, *Trio Sonata in C* creeps into the air, popping and scratchy, the high thin notes of the organ lost in the hum of the speakers.

From Thee to My Sole Self

At this age, nothing is easy. I prop my newspaper against the back of the other kitchen chair, mornings; it's so hard to keep my hands from trembling. That's merely a nuisance, of course. The big danger is falling. I've developed an intuition for handholds and soft landing spots. It's not a pleasant feeling, this knowledge that when the brain sends down a message—*lift that foot, turn this way*—the body may be asleep at the switch. It's as if my body is an empty house inhabited by a ghost who flits from floor to floor, rattling windows and slamming cupboard doors.

My daughter, LuAnn, stops by once a week, on Fridays when she drops Patty off at "the rat's." Actually, she and her ex-husband are on friendly terms, but she still always calls him the rat when Patty's not around, partly as a joke and partly out of habit. I enjoy our Friday evenings together; they give me an excuse to fix something nice, though LuAnn always protests and insists on doing the dishes afterward. "Mo-*therr*," she scolds when she comes in the door and smells a ham in the oven, but I think she enjoys it too. I don't think she eats well enough, but I'm tactful enough not to ask.

As the years go by, I get closer to the belief that LuAnn is Marshall's child, not my husband's. Marshall and I weren't together long; in Piedmont, you can feel the talk closing in on you before you even do anything. But in those few weeks of furtive, fevered imagining of impossible things, somebody became a father. All the old gossips around town could count, and I could count, and Richard could count, and everyone in Piedmont practiced their arithmetic when I turned up pregnant.

I couldn't tell it myself, at first. Her hair was brown—good; but it was straight. Her eyes were dark, but then again, so were my mother's. She was neither short and stocky like Richard nor tall and slim like Marshall. But now I watch her and I think I know. She's forty-five now, almost the same age Marshall was when he left town. I notice her easy conversation, the way she walks into a room looking straight ahead. Sometimes Marshall would be in a room ten minutes before turning around from whoever he was talking with to see who else was there.

She brings me something every Friday, magazines or library books. She thinks I should sell the house because I might break a hip on the stairs or have a sunstroke in the garden. Perhaps she thinks those ideas never occur to me, when in fact they take up much of my time. But keeling over in the garden is as good a way to die as any. Come to think of it, I'd like to die in the garden with a hoe in my hand. I'd just as soon be buried out there too, but of course that would leave an empty plot beside Richard. How they would talk then! Half the tombstone eternally unfinished, "Richard (1935-1998)" on one side and "Beryl (1939-)" on the other. The immortal woman.

My husband loved me, but after the first few years he didn't love me very much. That was the way we were then; the husband went about his business, the wife went about hers, and you didn't talk of love. Richard had a tie yard to run. He wanted a wife who would be an asset, who would hold office in the Bay View Club and Eastern Star, someone to organize church banquets. I didn't let him down. I was president of the club in 1988 and Grand Matron of the star that same year. Marshall was his office manager, Marshall the noble sufferer with the crippled wife. He was the one who talked of love.

LuAnn tells me she has a boyfriend now. What a silly word. People stop having boyfriends when they're sixteen. But I suppose it sounds better than "lover."

"I want you to meet Dennis one of these days," she told me last week.

"What does this Dennis do?" I asked. We were in the garden and she was trying to get me to come inside and talk. Anything to get that hoe out of my hands.

"He's a pretty important man," she said. "He works for the hat factory, in the office."

"Are you going to get married?"

"Oh, *married*," she said, as if she'd never thought of it before. "We're not really at that stage in our relationship yet." She wants to get married in the worst way.

"Then why do you want me to meet him?"

"I just think you'd like him."

She wants me to die happy, knowing that my daughter will be married to a nice man who wears a tie at the hat factory and orders a hundred uneducated women around. Richard wore a tie, too. Every morning he'd put on a clean white shirt and a necktie and drive to the yards before dawn. He was the first man there every day for forty years, and made it a point of pride to count every log that came in and every crosstie that went out. The loggers hated him. With Torrance, the other sawmiller in town, they could bring in a load right at quitting time and then haul it out again. They knew Torrance never missed his dinner. In the morning, they'd bring the same load in again and get paid for it twice.

LuAnn shouldn't have stayed here. She should have moved to Little Rock, or at least Jonesboro. This town is for old people like me who don't mind doing nothing, who chart their courses through their own living rooms like sailing ships navigating reefs, waiting to fall and break a bone. LuAnn has outgrown this town, like a catfish in a guppy bowl—after you get a certain size, you can't even turn around anymore.

I wonder how much she remembers about growing up here. Some evenings when she was a baby, Richard would pick her up and gaze at her, not speaking. She would begin to squirm and cry almost immediately—his hands were so large and unfamiliar—but

Richard held on. He carried her like you carry a strange cat, one hand on top and one hand below. After a few moments, he would put her down again.

I tried to make up for his lack of love, but of course that never works. I kissed her every morning, and hugged her when she went off to school, and kissed her every bedtime. I should have realized that she'd fall in love with the first boy that kissed her, before she could find out that the one kiss means you're safe and the other kiss means you're lost.

Patty is thirteen now, a much prettier girl than LuAnn or I ever was. Children grow up so fast these days. She's worn a bra for years and tells me—me, her grandma—about kissing boys. LuAnn is making the same mistake, always hugging her, combing her hair, smoothing her clothes, until I want to shout *Stop, get your hands off her, remember the rat.* But that wouldn't work either. We all find our own rats to love.

Patty stays the night with me every couple of months, whenever LuAnn and her new Dennis have some special occasion that won't wait until the weekend. We spend the morning getting dirty in the garden, then take long hot baths in the afternoon. We get out my photo albums and make fun of the people in the pictures, how stiff they look, how oddly dressed. Or we turn on the television and make fun of those people.

"Who's that, Grandma?" she asked one night.

It was the group picture at the annual pancake breakfast in '65 or '66. And for a moment I felt the room rise up, felt like some melodrama heroine with a family curse: her pointing finger rested on Marshall, his head bobbed up above everyone else's, his straight black hair combed back, his black eyes looking out at us, sharp. "That was your grandfather's office manager for many years."

"He's *handsome.*"

I wanted to turn the page. The picture was yellow and cracked, one of those old Brownie snapshots with scalloped edges. But those eyes! Turn the page. "I'm sure there must be handsome boys at your school."

"Just old Darrell Finch, and he's so dorky. He thinks he's great."

She went on to other pictures, drawing her feet up underneath her on the sofa and reading the captions LuAnn had written so painstakingly as a child, white ink on the stiff black pages.

"Whatever happened to him?" she murmured.

"He moved to Indiana a few years after that picture."

"To buy his own sawmill?"

"No, dear. He took up farming."

I should have known that would perk her up, "Farming? Why'd he do that?"

"Oh, it's a long story." I thought to let it drop there, but Patty, crafty Patty, is like her mother. She knows when secrets are being withheld. So I surrendered before a shot was fired, answering her long pause and furtive glance, and said, "There was a scandal with one of the women in our church and he had to leave town."

"Really? Tell me about it."

"There's really nothing to tell, dear."

"Please?"

"That's all there is to the story. It became known that he was involved with one of the ladies, and he left town," I said, turning on the television.

The rat, I wanted to say. I waited ten years, waiting for his poor cripple Margery to finally die, waiting for Richard to get caught under a runaway load of logs, deceiving myself long after I stopped deceiving my husband, and instead Marshall got caught in the church basement with Marie Michaels. Caught with her, swearing the same things that he swore to me when I was young and attracttive. He loves you dearly, but his poor sick wife can't stand the strain and needs care in these final years.

Marshall is ten years dead now, and poor sick Margery is still living in a rest home in Elkhart, the last I heard. Oh yes, he was handsome, I wanted to shout. I wanted to seize Patty and shake her till her braces rattled and say to her, listen, this is how it is. You're beautiful and you like to be kissed. And one day you look around and dorky old Darrell Finch has eyes like a god. He kisses you and you feel like an ice cream cone, you want him to turn you around and around, slurping you up as you melt.

But I didn't say it, of course. I settled back on the sofa and put my arm around my lovely young granddaughter and watched television comedies while I remembered the church socials and pancake breakfasts. When LuAnn was young we always went to the Wednesday night dinners. She and Marshall's little Beth were play-mates, almost the same age, and had drawn a hopscotch court on the sidewalk in front of the church. We'd be in the basement for dinner and hear them through the window, heels tapping, counting. They'd stay out there until it was time to go.

Richard watched them, of course. He watched and watched them, his eyes as opaque and impassive as if he were calculating the board feet in a load of oak. Once, after a church supper, we were carrying our dishes out to the car when he interrupted their hop-scotch. "Come here, hon," he said to Marshall's little girl, whose birth—it was said—was the straw that broke poor Margery's health.

He squatted down and tried to put a note of warmth into his voice. "You're Mr. Green's little girl, aren't you? Come here. What's your name, hon?"

She was frightened but obedient. "Beth."

"Beth? That's a pretty name. How old are you, Beth?" He put his arm around her.

"Five. Almost five."

"Almost five? Why, you're a big girl. My LuAnn is only five and a half, and you're just as tall as she is. Come here, LuAnn. You girls stand back to back and let's see who's tallest. That's right. Well, LuAnn, you're a little bit taller, but not much."

He held them together and peered into their faces. His white shirt glowed under the streetlight. "Now let's see which one is prettiest." They giggled and tried to twist away, but he held them tight. "You sure have pretty eyes, Beth, but let's see, LuAnn has pretty eyes too. How about the hair?" he said, passing his hand over their little heads. "I just don't know. Maybe we can tell by the hands. Hold out your hands—"

"Stop! Will you stop!" I shouted. The dishes crashed to the sidewalk from my hands. I tried to beat his broad white back, but he leaped to his feet and seized my hands, gripping them so hard I felt my wrists would break. I heard chairs scoot in the church basement as people came to the windows.

"Pack up the dishes," he said. I did, holding back tears. The girls had run out into the dark behind a tree. Richard turned to the people craning their necks up through the window wells. "No problem. She just dropped the dishes."

I thought about that moment for a long time that night, while Patty gradually fell asleep against my shoulder and people on the television laughed and laughed. LuAnn tells me I live too much in the past, and she's right, as usual. Why shouldn't I live in the past? There have been two men that I've loved and hated and come to forgive, but they're dead now, in the past. My hands tremble. My sleep is fitful and light; I wake in the night and listen. My bushes brush against my bedroom window. I live in an empty house.

The Fair

Mary Beth lay in the soft grass on the hillside of the park, halfway between the row of picnic tables and pavilions that strung along the top of the ridge and the level ground of the valley, where the fair had been set up. Music from the carnival floated up, reduced by distance to little more than a tuneless grate that would have been incomprehensible had she not known it from repetition on the local classic rock station. Her dad's music, or maybe even her grandpa's. *I love rock'n'roll. Put another dime in the jukebox, baby.* Dimes and jukeboxes, sure.

She was supposed to wait ten minutes before walking back to the fair, as she and Denny had agreed, for they knew that showing up together, or even in close proximity, would set off a chain of talk that neither of them wanted to deal with. So she looked up at the stars and tried to count to a hundred, until she lost track and stopped.

All along the waterfall with you. My brown-eyed girl.

Mary Beth was a brown-eyed girl, although she couldn't imagine anyone writing a song about her. She liked her hair, which was long and easy to manage, although she wished it had a little curl, but her eyes were too big for her face, and her body felt out of proportion. She didn't regret letting Denny touch her, down there, even though he was a boy she had no plans for and was, as her mom would say, not their kind of people. He was a sweet guy, affectionate, and she knew she could count on him not to blab. So what if it hadn't been a magical occasion? She'd had to move his hand to the right place, and even then had felt only a pleasant sensation, nothing grand or transporting to treasure in her memory, just the strange experience of another person messing around in her private spaces.

And then when she had done her part, she had only gripped him for a little while, feeling the curious spongy hardness of him, like a heavily padded steering wheel, before he groaned and arched his back, and made his mess. Then he was gone, with only the barest of affectionate mumbles.

Which reminded her: She needed to wash her hands. She could still feel the goo on her hand, or at least imagined that she could.

We will, we will, rock you. We will, we will, rock you.

Which reminded her: Had she put out water for Bonnie? That had been her excuse to leave the family camper this evening, not that she had really needed one, since it was understood that kids could roam the midway till closing time as long as they didn't get in someone's car and go out driving. And she remembered the entire familiar routine, scattering new straw, brushing out Bonnie's wool, and refreshing her water trough. But had she? Or was she remembering that from yesterday? It was always the same, every day, and today she had been preoccupied with herself, amazed at her own boldness in kissing Denny Wallace behind their trailer that afternoon and agreeing to meet him on the hillside tonight. And now she couldn't recall whether she had gone through the routine, or just imagined it.

Mary Beth sat up in the fragrant grass and tried to think. It was all so real, the smell of the barn, the musky sweetness of Bonnie's wool, the scratch of the straw. But had she really done it? Suddenly she doubted. Mr. Macalester, the barnmaster, would yell at her if she came out to the barn after all the sheep had bedded down and risked disturbing them on the night before the show. The kids all laughed behind Mr. Macalester's back at his grouchy posturing; he was like the little bulldog she saw from the bus every morning as they drove by the neighbor's place, all bark and bluster. But up close he scared her. She didn't like the idea of facing a scolding from him in the dim solitude of the sheep barn.

But she couldn't let Bonnie go through the night without water. She'd never sleep for worrying. She had to go to the barn.

Harvey Macalaster was in no mood for anybody's bullshit. He said the words aloud to himself as if for practice, muttering them low so he wouldn't stir the animals: "I am in no mood for your bullshit." Not that there was an object for his mood yet, but one would likely show itself soon enough.

Harvey understood the need for a carnival at the fair. It drew the town kids and their parents, and the out-of-county people, and Harvey had been on the Fair Board long enough to know that the money the carnival brought in was what kept them afloat, no matter what the ag companies and local businesses donated. And they had been working with Bowman Amusements for as long as he could remember. But ever since the old man died and the boys took over, the quality of the carnies had unmistakably declined, in his opinion. The idea of quality carnies sounded like a contradiction. The old-time carnies were hard-working guys down on their luck, though, and they knew Old Man Bowman would bounce them out without a penny if they showed up drunk. Not like the current bunch of no-goods, who stank of alcohol and looked hopped-up all the time, with their sleeve tattoos and scraggly beards.

He'd caught two of the sons-of-bitches last year, trying to sneak into the sheep barn to do God knows what, shoot their drugs or drink, or maybe even smoke, in a barn full of hay and straw and live animals. Or cut the animals' throats just for fun. He'd heard a story about something like that, some nutcase in Kentucky who got high on something and killed a whole field full of Simmental cattle. Harvey had been carrying his pistol that night and held the two carnies at gunpoint until the youngest Bowman boy had come to fetch them. And they had looked at him as if *he* was the wrongdoer, and Bowman had said, "You fellas know better than to wander off into the arena area," and took them away without so much as a thank-you.

That wouldn't happen this year. He had already spoken with Howell Adams, the deputy, a man who shared his opinion of the carnies. If he caught anybody this year, he would not call Bowman. He would call Howell, and have them taken to jail, and by God he would press charges. Harvey had been the barnmaster at the sheep barn since 1982, when old Knudsen died, and there would be no slacking of standards on his watch.

Knudsen. Now there was an old-school sheepman. Immigrant parents who had herded sheep on the rocky mountainsides of Norway, where wolves and storms and bitter cold were a sheepman's education. Knudsen stuck with the old breeds and simple ways, and even Harvey thought him overly stubborn with the Extension people and the articles in *Sheep Industry News* that spoke of new methods. He remembered visiting Knudsen once when the old man was dealing with a belligerent Cheviot ram. "Here's how you stop that shit," Knudsen said. He drew the ram into his loading chute, then tripped it, stood on its neck, and pissed into its nostrils, a whole bladder full, and didn't stop until he was empty, no matter how much the ram bleated and struggled. Then he turned it loose to run into the field. "He knows who's boss now. Every time he smells me coming, he'll tremble like a baby." When Knudsen died, he left his farm to the Lutheran Church, even though he had always said that the local bunch were Saxon Lutherans and thus apostates, more or less.

Old Knudsen had been an oddball and a harsh judge at events, scaring the 4-H kids half to death, but every year the sheep barn ran with smooth efficiency, the stalls scrubbed down and strawed, electricity and fresh water in proper order, ribbons and prizes arranged, and plenty of sweet hay to keep even the pickiest breed content. The least Harvey could do was maintain that standard. Any lowlife who thought he could disturb the orderly operation of the sheep barn would have to answer to Harvey Macalester.

In the center of the barn, Harvey kept an enormous metal desk, donated by an office supply store back in the days when there was still an office supply store in town, which he called his command center. As the long summer twilight lapsed into darkness, Harvey settled into his desk chair. He opened the top right drawer, checked his pistol, and slid the drawer shut again. Now all he had to do was stay awake.

Kelso didn't think much of this fair. At the bigger ones, Gasconade County or Warren County, there would be a show on Saturday night, and even during work he could hear some of the performance. But these little county fairs couldn't afford a big-name singer like Trace Adkins or Charlie Daniels. They had to make do with local talent and a demolition derby. On the bright side, a lame show meant more business on the midway, proportionally speaking.

Bowman had already passed his booth twice, making his stupid fingers-to-the-eyes, I'm-watching-you gesture that he had seen in a movie somewhere, as if Kelso didn't know he was being watched after the incident in Salem. Kelso knew when they set up in Salem that he would have trouble. There was a late-night bar right down the road, within walking distance of their trailers, and he felt an overpowering thirst. And sure enough he ended up there after the fair closed down, and within a half hour he was trading punches with some logger in the parking lot, until the logger went after a shotgun in the back of his truck, the Salem PD turned up, and things very nearly got serious. And of course the carny never gets the benefit of the doubt. Kelso was still working off his bail money from that little adventure, and would be for another week at least.

So, the middle of nowhere was fine. Less opportunity for outside trouble, and the boys all knew that a bottle in your trailer meant immediate dismissal. He could live with that state of affairs.

Besides, the middle of nowhere felt like home territory. He'd grown up in a small town and had trained at Fort Lost-in-the-Woods, so when he was discharged he landed back there, half by chance and half by instinct. But he hadn't adjusted well to work at the boat factory, and the next job he found, working the pit at the Jiffy Lube, left him filthy and aching at the end of the day, his shoulders in agony from the overhead work. So last year when he drifted away from the truck pulls at the Laclede County Fair, strolling the midway in search of anything interesting, he ended up leaning against the guy rope of a booth, talking with Bowman, and the next thing he knew he had a booth and bunk of his own.

The only problem was the boredom of it all, calling out to the passing dopes to entice them into the game, the inane banter they exchanged. *Look,* he wanted to tell them, *you're here to spend money and I'm here to take it. Let's just cut the shit.* But oh no, that wouldn't do, so he had to yap with them and draw them in. The customers expected it, Bowman said, so they all had to keep up a patter. Customers. Leave it to Bowman to call a mark a "customer." But oh, he had a business degree from college, so he was a genius. And it wasn't even real money, but red tickets they bought from the cashier's booth, which gave the whole interaction an unreal quality, fake money changing hands for fake prizes.

Kelso kept his opinions to himself. The carny life agreed with him, and Bowman wasn't a bad guy, altogether. He'd bailed him out of Salem and a couple of other places; name a boss in the real world who would do such a thing for a low-ass game operator. Others might sneer at a debt of loyalty, but not Kelso.

So he stood at his counter and called out to the chumps. His big prize was an enormous stuffed Simba, and although *The Lion King* had been out for what, fifteen, eighteen years, the girls still loved it. All these high school ballplayers who thought they were so skilled just stood there and flung him ticket after ticket. That fucking lion was not going home with any of them, although Kelso made sure everybody left with one of the forty-nine-cent plush toys that festooned the third row of the wall behind him.

And there came one now, a big, bulgy-armed kid who looked to be about seventeen and who clearly spent too much time in the high school gym trying to build up his biceps, with a determined look on his face and a roll of tickets in his hand.

"Is this a fair game?" the kid said.

"Of course it's a fair game," said Kelso. He took a wooden hoop off the counter and slipped it over one of the blocks that held a prize. It fell over the prize easily, of course, as it always did when dropped from straight above. A carny trick so old it had whiskers, Kelso knew, and judging from the look on the kid's face he knew it too.

"All right," he said, and slapped down five tickets. "I'm gonna win me that lion. I know a girl who would just love to have that lion."

I bet you do, Kelso thought, and as he leaned forward to take the tickets, he smelled the unmistakable aroma of fresh sex. *This son-of-a-bitch has been out getting himself laid,* and the idea made him resentful at the smug doofus in his team roster T-shirt, strolling the midway after getting his jollies, and made him ever more determined that the Lion King would never come down from his hook.

A dollar per ticket, and twenty tickets later the kid had won nothing. Kelso kept his voice friendly. "Let me guess," he said. "Linebacker?"

"How'd you know?"

Because you're not coordinated enough to play offense, you're too small for the line, and you're not fast enough for the corner. "Just a guess. You've got that killer instinct."

The kid looked peevish but had nothing to complain about. Kelso held out another hoop.

"I'm out of tickets. You stay right here."

He dashed off toward the cashier's kiosk. Kelso thought about calling after him, *Stay right here? Where else would I be?* but decided not to inflame things. He glanced across the midway to the old lady in the cotton candy booth, who grinned at him.

At the end of his counter stood a girl he had not noticed before, leaning on her elbows. She looked to be about twenty, full-on Goth or at least trying to be, with dyed black hair, heavy eyeliner, and a black outline around her lipstick. She wore a T-shirt under a long-sleeved thin plaid cotton shirt, and Kelso struggled to keep his eyes from straying to the body underneath the T-shirt, which was a good body indeed.

"That looked like fun," she said.

"What?"

"Taking all of that asshole's tickets."

"I didn't take them, he gave them to me willingly. And how do you know he's an asshole? He could be a real sweetheart when you get to know him." Kelso pulled his fingers through his thin blond hair, which he now wished he had washed.

"He's an asshole. He's in my little brother's class." She swirled the hoops on the counter, stacking them into intricate patterns then spreading them out again. "I like your piercings."

"Oh yeah?" He fingered the three rings in the upper part of his left ear, the end product of a day's celebration when he got his discharge papers from the Army. "I've had second thoughts from time to time." A kid dismounted from Pharoah's Fury and sprinted toward the Port-O-Lets, looking stricken. "What's your name, anyway?"

"Daphne." She glanced up at him through mascara-matted eyelashes with a guarded expression, as if expecting to be mocked.

"Cool! Daphne like in *Scooby-Doo?*"

"I guess. Maybe." She shrugged. "My mom was a fan."

"Daphne was the hot one, so cool. I'm Rob." It sounded strange to say the name, for around the carnival he was always just Kelso, and he only saw his first name on his Friday paycheck. That line about Daphne in the cartoon seemed too forward, on second thought, and he regretted it. But too late now.

He handed her a hoop. "Want to try it?"

She gave it an awkward fling and missed everything. "I suck at games."

"Everybody throws too hard. It's like darts. You have to use a light touch."

He picked up a hoop and tossed it, and sure, it wasn't fair because he was closer, but even so it felt like the perfect throw, floating like a Frisbee, and it settled over a prize without catching on any corner of the block. As if the universe was trying to help him out for once. And yes he was showing off for a girl, but so what. Daphne said a quiet "Yay!" and even clapped a little.

In the distance he could see high-school-hero approaching, a new wad of tickets in his hand. "Listen," he said. "I'm working right now but the midway closes in a few minutes. Do you want to hang out later, maybe?"

"Sure. My mom and I have a booth." She nodded toward the area near the entrance, where the locals had a cluster of pop-up canopies.

"Oh yeah? How come I've never seen you before?"

"We only do this one fair 'cause it's in our town. Most weekends we both have to work."

"Okay. Where can I find you?"

"Just come to the booth. My mom's cool. We'll be tearing down." She twisted her ring. "We sell artwork and stuff. Don't laugh."

"I wouldn't dream of it! I love art."

"It's wolves and things like that. Sunsets."

"I think that's fantastic." Now it was his turn for a revealing. "You should know, um—" He cleared his throat. "I have a kind of substance abuse problem, so I try to stay away from—you know— situations—"

"I get it," Daphne said. "I'm not the big party girl myself. Just me and my mom, our dogs, our paints." To take the awkwardness out of the moment, she pointed to the big lion. "They sell those at Dollar General, you know."

"Where do you think we buy them?"

They both laughed at this, the absurdity of the whole enterprise, and she reached over and tapped his forearm. "Don't stand me up, now. I'll be waiting."

"I won't." And with that, she was gone into the milling herd on the midway, and Kelso couldn't believe his good fortune that an actual pretty girl had come up to talk to him, and that she had agreed to meet him later, and he realized that he needed to wash up and brush his teeth. The kid slapped his tickets on the counter with a fierce look, but Kelso didn't mind. He might even give him a few pointers to help him win. The world felt enlarged.

Leanne Whitehead knew that Mary Beth was a good girl, one who could be trusted to make the right decisions, but she also knew that a girl could find herself in a situation without ever having made a decision, like a mouse in a funnel trap, led on by nothing more than the desire for movement until she was wedged into a place where it was impossible to turn around. "Let her have her fun, she's just a kid," Royal told her, but being a man, he had little notion of the price tag of fun. So here Leanne stood on the midway, with no clear idea about where to look or what to say if she found her. Mary Beth would be embarrassed to see her, even mortified, but Leanne couldn't help herself. Perhaps it was a mother's job to feel fear for those who didn't have sense to be afraid themselves.

She would head for the sheep barn since there might be something the matter with Bonnie that would have kept Mary Beth there so long. Mary Beth doted on that creature like a mother herself, and this was the year that they hoped to qualify for state. And if she wasn't in the barn—

Alcohol. Drug-using kids in her class. Predatory strangers. Late-night joyrides in somebody's car, with an inattentive driver sending text messages.

Worry was her constant condition, worry that blended into fear so seamlessly that she might as well call it that. Worry, anxiety, fear: whatever the word, it owned her. She liked to imagine that it would leave once Mary Beth went off to college in another year, but she knew in her heart that this hope was vain.

So when would it leave? Never, she supposed. Leanne had considered telling her doctor about her constant feeling of dread, but being an anxious mother felt like her fate, and she had a hard time imagining any other version of herself. Anxious mother, anxious mother on medication, not much distance between them.

She saw Howell Adams, the deputy, standing near the Pork Producers' Building, but wasn't so foolish as to go talk to him. He would listen and nod, and promise to look into it, and then as soon as she was out of sight he would chuckle to himself at the mom with her crazy fears. She'd seen that before. Didn't he watch the news these days? Royal still humored her like that sometimes, though he had learned to curb the impulse. So she would complete a sweep of the fairgrounds, check the sheep barn, and only then would she think about talking to Howell.

She could text, of course, or call. But she had been there before, the unwanted call, the poorly timed text. The rolling of eyes that would follow, Royal tap-dancing around the question of whether she was an overprotective fool, Mary Beth walking around for the rest of the day with a wounded look. She would stay off the phone unless the fear overwhelmed her. No law enforcement, no calling or texting. She was alone in this.

Leanne tried to stay nonchalant as she walked the midway, her head swiveling. None of Mary Beth's usual friends came into view; no surprise, as most of them were town kids and, if they came to the fair at all, were likely to be bunched up in the lines for the thrill rides. But there was Dennis Wallace, one of her gang, bellied up to a counter at one of the carnival booths and pitching hoops as though lives were at stake.

She eased herself beside him and waited to speak until he had made his throw. A scary-looking carnival worker watched with an unreadable expression. Finally, he tossed the hoop, missed, and muttered a curse word.

"Hello, Dennis!" she said, making her voice brighter than her feelings. "Trying your luck?"

He leaped as if she had struck him. "Mrs. Whitehead! You're out late."

"I thought I'd walk a little before bedtime." Leanne tried to sound casual. "Have you seen Mary Beth around?"

"Um, no. Not lately." He wouldn't meet her eyes. Did he know something? Was some kind of party going on somewhere? "I saw her about half an hour ago. She was just strolling along, having fun."

She didn't believe him, with his twitchy body and sideways looks. Leanne waited a few moments to see if he would say more. That had been her dad's trick when she was young, just stand there mute until her own discomfort made her blurt out whatever she had been holding back. But this kid had more practice in the art of concealment. He stood there looking empty.

"Was she with anyone?" She knew she was prying. But so what? He was lying, which was worse.

Dennis squinted and looked off into the distance, pretending to think. "I don't think so. I think she was headed to the barn. If I see her, I'll tell her you're looking for her." Leanne fought back the impulse to shout at him.

"All right, thanks. I'm not really looking for her, I'm just—" She turned away. Nothing left to say.

"Mrs. Whitehead?" Leanne stopped and waited, hopeful. "Does Mary Beth like Elsa, you know, the girl in *Frozen?*"

"I don't know. I suppose she does."

Dennis gestured to the back wall of the booth, where a figurine of Elsa in her sweeping blue cloak was zip-tied, along with two dozen other trinkets and prizes. "I won anything on the second row. I was hoping to win one of the big ones on the top row, but I don't think that's in the picture." He glanced at the carny with a grimace. "Anyway, I thought Mary Beth might like that Elsa, um, statue."

"I'm sure she would." Leanne didn't know what else to say, so she walked away. This boy wanted to win her daughter a prize at a carnival game. What was that supposed to mean? She could hear Royal now, with his "let the kids have their fun" talk, but Royal had no notion, none whatsoever. She had better things in mind for Mary Beth than to be wooed by children's toys, especially ones from this near-roughneck whose highest accomplishment, so far, was the quarterback sack at Iberia that preserved the win at sectionals.

Had Mary Beth encouraged this boy somehow? If so, she needed to have a serious conversation with her, a real heart-to-heart about her future and the choices she needed to make to achieve it. No disrespect to this Dennis Wallace, but Mary Beth was in the top five of her class, with thoughts of veterinary school or a future in science, unlike this young man, whose chief ambition as far as she knew was to follow his dad into the Highway Department.

Behind her, she heard the carny say, "Make your choice, man. We're shutting down." As she walked, booths turned off their lights, rides came to a stop, and the music turned silent. Everyone except her was drifting toward the parking lot.

Leanne stopped and took a breath. She was overreacting, she knew she was overreacting, but she couldn't help herself. She needed to see Mary Beth, to know she was all right, to silence the racket inside her spinning brain. Just let her find Mary Beth, she prayed silently, and she would leave this business with the boy for another, quieter, time.

*   *   *

Harvey Macalaster dreamed about the day he came home from ag school during the Christmas break of his sophomore year, the year he had pretty much decided to quit. The war was escalating big-time by then. At the ag school, unlike the rest of the campus, the boys didn't march around and throw things, and some of them had even given up their student deferments and enlisted. Harvey felt discontented and left behind. His classes seemed abstract and dull, even the ag ones, and he had written his thoughts to his parents.

His father met him at the bus station. He glanced at Harvey's blue jeans and flannel shirt, and said, "Glad you don't have on your nice clothes. You can help me hay the Hallweks' cattle on our way home."

He said no more, not that he needed to. Everybody knew Bobby Hallwek had gone to the war and gotten killed, and that the Hallweks were having a tough time of it, especially Mrs. Hallwek, who didn't emerge from their house anymore but kept a pot of coffee brewing for the neighbor farmers who came by daily to tend the herd while the Hallweks mourned. When they reached the Hallweks' turnoff, his father drove past the house straight to the barn, backed into the hayloft, and pulled a couple of pairs of leather gloves from beneath the truck seat. "We need ten bales," he said.

And though they were sheep people, Harvey and his dad knew enough about cattle farming to hay the herd properly, scattering the hay from the back of their pickup at intervals across the field so the cattle wouldn't bunch up and fight over the best bits, and to ensure that their manure would be spread more widely across the pasture. When they finished, they drove past the house again without stopping.

"We'll pay them a visit another time. Your mother would skin us if she found out we dawdled on our way home."

So as they passed, they waved at the ravaged Mrs. Hallwek, peeking out from behind her kitchen curtains, and Harvey knew that they would not speak about his idea of quitting school. There was no need. No reason for his father to turn to him and say, "Is this what you want to happen to your mother? To become a haunted soul, unable to step outside her house? Do you want us to have to rely on our neighbors to care for the farm, knowing that eventually we will have to throw in the towel as we grow old and their concern fades?" No need to say it, because Harvey knew it already, and he knew that he would be going back to school to slog through his classes and keep his deferment, and that after school he'd come back to the farm and apply for a 2-C agricultural exemption. Because he was needed. The country needed soldiers, but the farm needed him.

In his dream he was back there in that pasture with his dad, tossing out the hay, but he was his current age and barely able to lift a bale. But because he was near the boundary between sleeping and waking, he knew it was a dream. He knew his father and mother had long since passed away, and the Hallweks, all of them sleeping at Mount Pisgah along with Bobby and half his high school class. He knew he'd done his duty and stayed on the farm, and that except for occasional trips to Springfield, and to St. Louis and Kansas City once a year to see a ballgame, and the cruise he'd gone on with the missus when he hit sixty-five, he'd never really left it. To some people, such a fate might seem sad, but in his dream he was happy, pulling bales off the tailgate and scattering the hay while his dad crept along in granny low. At the time he had felt miserable and frustrated, but in the dream he wanted to tell his dad that it was all right, that everything had turned out all right, but as always in a dream, he was unable to speak.

Mary Beth had indeed watered Bonnie, as she knew in her heart she had done. She guessed her anxiety had come from guilt at being out with Denny doing forbidden things, and she had felt an impulse to be right and responsible again. Bonnie was asleep in a corner of her pen, and all of Mary Beth's tools and supplies were in their right place. She unfolded a metal chair in the opposite corner and sat down, in no hurry to leave.

She had so feared coming to the sheep barn and facing Mr. Macalester, but when she arrived, he was leaned back in his office chair, snoring like a rhinoceros, his mouth gaped wide. It was such a funny sight! She had thought about taking a picture with her phone, but the flash would have awakened him. Besides, anyone she sent the photo to might have reposted it, and she didn't want to cause him any embarrassment. So she had tiptoed past. She would keep the memory to herself and bring it back the next time she felt intimidated.

Her own mind, though, was racing. She needed to let it slow down. It wasn't so much the physical act that had set her mind churning, for they had not gone too far at all, and Denny had not tried to pressure her across a boundary, though she could sense his immense craving. That was the exciting thing: to be wanted that much, to be the object of such craving. It made her feel powerful, and she could understand why some girls fell victim to that sensation, to be *wanted* so badly, that they ended up doing foolish things.

But she couldn't think too much about that now. She had to-morrow to consider, calculating how much time she needed for the shampoo, conditioning, blow drying, and final trim so that she finished just moments before it was time to lead Bonnie into the ring. But she couldn't hurry it, for Bonnie detected her moods and would become hard to handle if she felt rushed. So it all had to be calm, smooth, but fast. She would rehearse it in her mind tonight and again in the morning, and she had no room for distractions.

As if on cue, her phone vibrated: a text from Denny.

Ur mom is out looking for you.

Oh, lordy. She should have thought. Of course Mom would be out looking, all worked up, because Mom got worked up over everything.

And now a second text:

Can I c u ltr 2nite?

She took one last look around the pen, her place of refuge. In the pen with Bonnie she was in charge, but outside she was just another kid, and it would be time for Mom's Quiz Bowl, lightning round. She wanted to go over and hug Bonnie. She was such a sweet sheep, and she could tell that Bonnie wanted to do well in a show. There was just something about her that Mary Beth felt, an eagerness to please, almost like a dog. She wanted to hug her and bury her face in her fragrant wool, but of course that would waken and upset Bonnie. So she folded up the chair, lifted it over the fence, and climbed out quietly.

She texted Denny back, and because those abbreviations had always seemed silly to her, she took care to write out every word. Who was so pressed for time that they couldn't spell a word? *Not tonight. Maybe tomorrow.* The presumption of it, thinking that she would try to sneak out of their camper to see him in the middle of the night, when he knew that tomorrow was show day.

And just as quietly, she slipped past Mr. Macalester's desk, not really tiptoeing, just placing one foot softly down on the packed dirt and then the next, suppressing a laugh at his outrageous snoring. Until the moment when, as she felt herself safe at last, the phone in her pocket rang with its insistent, unmistakable ringtone, the ringtone she had assigned only to Mom.

Kelso had barely dropped the awning on the front of his booth when Daphne appeared again. "I thought I was going to come to you," he said.

Daphne frowned. "My mom got mad and left. She told the people at the next booth that we weren't selling anything anyway, and I was off running around instead of working, so she packed up the trailer and went home." She was trying to keep her face calm, but every few seconds she drew in her lower lip and chewed it.

"Look, I know we've just met, but do you think you could give me a ride home?"

"Sure. No problem." His car was in the far back lot where the workers had to park, and he wasn't sure it would start without a jump, but he'd worry about those things when the time came. They walked down the empty midway as the lights blinked out, chunk by chunk.

As they walked, he let his hand dangle by his side in hopes that she would do the same. Sure enough, after a few steps their fingertips brushed. He took her hand.

The simple pleasure of this, holding hands while walking along the flat grassy ground, made him feel grand and expansive. Kelso fought back the impulse to skip. He didn't want to spoil whatever was between them by doing something stupid while she was upset.

"I'm sorry about this thing with your mom," he said.

Daphne shrugged. "She gets pissy. Can't blame her. I think she's more pissed that the artwork didn't sell than she is at me." She chuckled. "Chances are she'll be over it by the time we get home. She'll want to give you a big hug and hear your life story. Come to think of it, I'd be kind of interested in hearing it myself."

Kelso felt relieved at her optimistic tone. He moved to put his arm around Daphne, but she slid out of his grasp with a supple half-twist. "Easy, cowboy," she said.

Kelso was mortified. Ten seconds after he'd told himself not to do anything stupid, here he was. "I'm so sorry," he stammered. "I didn't mean—"

"It's okay. Let's just, you know, focus on first things first. Get home, patch things up with Mom, maybe see what's in the fridge."

He was about to apologize again, but she took his hand and they walked on.

That was when they heard somebody's phone ring, and a moment later the voice of a man shouting inside one of the animal barns. He sounded angry to the point of being unhinged, and his words were a messy jumble. Kelso and Daphne looked at each other.

"Guess we'd better check this out," Kelso said.

The animal barn was as dark as the inside of a sleeping bag, and it had the same warm, lived-in aroma. Kelso heard a second voice, not a shout but a loud whisper, a girl's voice.

The man shouted, "I have a gun! Don't come any closer!"

"Mr. Macalaster! Mr. Macalaster! It's me!" the girl whispered.

"I'm warning you!"

"Stop shouting! You'll frighten the sheep!" the girl said, urgent. And indeed there were stirrings and rustlings throughout the barn.

Oh shit, Kelso thought. *An old guy with a gun.* He didn't feel heroic, but Daphne gripped his hand and the girl's voice sounded frightened, so they crept forward.

The voices came from the center of the building, where the long entry aisle ended in some heaps that Kelso couldn't make out in the darkness; bales of hay or sacks of feed, he guessed. He groped for the chest-high railing of the stalls and followed it with his left hand while holding Daphne's with his right, keeping to the shadows.

Then the girl's phone rang again, and a woman ran up from behind them, out of the darkened midway where they had just come from, crying, "Baby! Baby! Are you all right?"

And in the darkness and her haste, she knocked into Daphne. It was a glancing blow but neither of them was prepared for it. They tumbled to the dirt with grunts of pain.

The light from the girl's phone screen illuminated the scene in a brief green wash: the old man and the girl, ten feet apart at the end of the aisle. But the sound of the collision made the girl drop the phone and run toward them, calling, "Mama! Is that you?" The old man turned to follow.

Kelso knelt and reached for Daphne, finding a shoulder. "Are you hurt?" he whispered.

"Nah."

So he stood up and spoke into the darkness in what he hoped was his most authoritative voice. "Everybody stop!"

In the silence that followed, he spoke more quietly. "The girl's right, we're scaring the sheep. Mister, are you all right?"

No reply.

"Okay, I'm going to turn on my phone so we don't trip over each other."

He switched on his phone's flashlight, and in its glare they all saw each other at last. The girl running toward them, distraught. The woman, who he recognized as the lady who had visited his booth at closing time, sprawled on the ground. The old man farther back with slumped shoulders, tears on his face, and no weapon in his hand. He had to admit, the old guy was a pretty good bluffer. Kelso helped Daphne to her feet, and the girl ran to her mother.

"I'm sorry," he told Daphne, thinking of the evening he had been anticipating, now busted, likely past repair. And she said, "No, I'm sorry," in return, and somehow that exchange triggered them all into apologizing, the girl saying *I'm sorry* and her mother saying *I'm sorry* as they knelt on the dusty floor, and the old fellow saying *I'm so sorry* to them all, saying it out into the broad air to everyone in general and no one in particular. But Kelso didn't feel a hundred percent sorry. He also felt a little light-headed, almost exhilarated, for he had managed to do something right for once in his life, and it was a beautiful summer evening, and they were at the fair.

The Trouble with Women

She said her name was Lori, and I didn't have no reason to doubt it, so Lori it was.

I ran across her at Darrell's Place, around nine o'clock last Wednesday night. Missouri is a hot place in the summer, hotter even in the way it feels at night than Oklahoma, where I also have lived, because it's a wet heat that you can't get off you. Darrell's Place in Redings Mill is out on Highway N-and-N, the old back road from Joplin to Neosho, and as you drive down the road you can see the heat rising up. When it rains, the rain will hit the pavement and turn to steam, and that's the truth.

I am not what you would call a handsome man. But I keep myself neat, I do not let myself "get seedy" like many of the divorced men I know, which accounts for my general success among the ladies, I think. I will be the first to tell you that I am shaped different from what I used to be, a bit of the "spare tire" on my middle, but that don't mean I can't keep myself sharp with the latest look and so forth. And the ladies appreciate that.

There was a bunch of boys from the La-Z-Boy plant playing pool in the back, so I thought at first maybe she was with them; but I didn't see no extra coasters, so I figured what the hell and sat down.

The first thing I see is that Lori is older than she looked from the bar, which was no real surprise because I guess everybody looks better at a distance. She's got her hair long and tied back in like a ponytail, which to me is peculiar in a woman maybe forty, forty-two years old. I mean after all.

But anyway, I sit down, we say hi.

"You a secretary?" I say.

"How did you know that? Do I look like a secretary?"

The answer, which I don't tell her, is yes and no. I always ask that question when I meet a new lady, cause maybe two-thirds of the time they *are* secretaries and they think you're some kind of Sherlock. But for her, yes she did look like a secretary, which is hard to explain except that they have a kind of pinchy, superior look about them, which of course you don't want to say to somebody. Give me an at-home lady any day.

So I say, "Not exactly, but I had you figured for a professional woman of some kind."

This perks her up, and I buy her a beer.

"You're a pretty good guesser," she says. "I am a secretary for Barks, Davis and Cornwell," with that be-impressed sound in her voice. The name means zip to me, but she says it's a law firm down-town. Well, well. The natural question is what is somebody with a downtown law firm doing out here on N-and-N, which I hate to call redneck territory but let's face facts. The short answer is she's thinking about getting laid, I think.

I am the purchasing agent for R-K-M, which is a millwork company here in town, and I do all right. Started in the warehouse and moved right on up. So I tell her about my job for a little bit. She looks good, a thoughtful kind of gal, and no fat on her, which is something I am not into.

We show each other some pictures of our kids. Mine are eighteen, seventeen, and twelve; hers is thirteen, stays with her dad in the summers. An oldest kid of thirteen makes me refigure. Could she be thirty-five, less maybe? Life is rough these days and it shows in people's faces.

She wants to talk about her divorce. The last thing I want to hear is how some man was a bum, but you sure can't say that, so the best thing to do is listen and nod. Which I do. You've heard it a million times—how it just wasn't working, the little girl, the try-once-more, the last straw.

"How long ago?" I say.

"Six months."

Those words are like the songs of angels in heaven to my ears. When you say six-month divorcee, you're talking about a woman who has an itch and is overdue to be scratched. To my mind, this game is over.

"The worst part was the actual court part," she says. "I had all the legal help I needed, of course, but that doesn't prepare you for actually getting up there and saying the things you have to say. It was so—"

"I know what you mean."

"So—"

Let's get off the divorce stuff, I want to say. Let's talk about the heat, or the ball team, or the tornado, or any old damn thing.

"So sad, you know, and final, permanent. This thing that you thought was going to be all of your life, it's canceled, and you're the one who's canceling it out. You know what the worst moment was?"

By now I'm busy studying the coaster.

"It was when it was all over with, and we were going down the hall, walking along, and I realized that up to now we always would have been side by side, even if we had just had a fight and weren't speaking. And I was behind him, and he kept walking faster, and I didn't want to catch up—we just got farther and farther apart down the hall. There was this awful moment when he got in the elevator, and I pretended to check my shoe because I couldn't—I didn't—" She stopped. "I'm sorry."

"That's okay."

"About a week later, I got a note in the mail. It was this little typed note that said, 'You are a plain woman, and no fun to be with.'"

We sit there for a while, pool balls cracking and a TV above the bar playing. She says after a while, "I started to laugh when I read it, and that was when I knew I was going to be all right."

So we laugh about it, and everything eases up. We talk more, and have another beer. I believe that when the time comes, you should not jack around, so after a while I take hold of her hand.

I say, "You are no plain woman. You're a terrific gal. I want you to come home with me."

This is a touchy moment most times. If they get shy and drop their heads, smile to themselves, I know I'm in. If they act surprised and get that shame-on-you look, it's still a maybe. But this gal, she just looks at me steady and straight, no change of expression, like she's looking in a mirror.

Finally she says: "Well, why not? I am a free woman, and I can do whatever I darn well feel like."

"That's the spirit," I say. "Here's to free women."

She smiles now and tips her glass to mine. They touch each other with a tiny little clink. Then into the parking lot—still hot, miserable hot—a quick smooch, into our cars, and home in a jiffy.

We go right upstairs to the bedroom and she turns her back to take off her clothes. That's okay, they're always embarrassed right then, and besides I was busy myself. Putting on one of them lubricateds, which I always use because you can never tell about people these days.

So we get on the bed and I slip it in, easy as pie. I am not bragging to tell you I have a good bit of "lasting power," you know, which the ladies like. I give her quite a ride and she took it real good.

Things are cozy and I'm about ready to drop off. But here something goes wrong, what it was I don't know. I never *said* anything to her that I can think of. Something gripes her, though, because she gets up and goes into the bathroom and is in there for a long time.

"Are you okay in there?" I call.

She says, "I'm all right," but doesn't come out. I think to myself, Don't let her be a weepy woman, Lord, save me from a weepy woman. After a while she comes back out and starts putting on her clothes.

"I'm going to go on home," she says, cool as can be.

I tell her, "Don't be silly. Crawl back in here."

"No, I want to go home." She's got her britches on, which is a pity.

"Come on back, baby." Women can act so crazy sometimes that you just want to tear your hair out.

I say, "What's the matter? Come and tell me." This is okay sometimes, they get a little sad afterwards and want you to hold them while they cry or tell you things. But this gal is not that type. She just looks glum.

I figure maybe I'll kid her some, cheer her up, and I say, "Lighten up, girl. What happened to my free woman?"

She just says, "You wouldn't understand."

She's got her shoes on, she's heading out the door. But now she stops. "I want fifty dollars," she says.

"Fifty dollars! For what?"

She waves her arm at the room. "For this."

I think to myself, well God damn. I didn't know whether the gal was a whore all along, or if she'd just decided to get into the business, or if she was playing me for a sucker, or what.

I said, "I didn't know you was a whore."

She said, "Me neither, until just now."

It didn't seem fair. I mean, you're supposed to tell a fellow. But what the hell, I've paid more for less. So I dug in my billfold and got her fifty.

Then a funny thing happens. I lay in bed listening to her find her way out—down the hall, then down the stairs, then fiddling with the front door lock—when I feel old Pete start to wake up under the covers. And in a couple of seconds I'm back in "season for pleasin'," as we say. I think about that gal and I don't know why, I just gotta get her back here with me. The car door shuts. I wrap the sheet around my middle and dash downstairs.

I look like some kind of escapee, but I don't care. I knock on the window three, four times before she rolls it down. The car is in reverse, but she's not pushing the pedal; it creeps down the driveway inch by inch.

I follow alongside.

"Please come back, baby."

She doesn't say anything. The car keeps rolling. Through the window, the streetlight cuts across her neck and shoulder, her hands kind of flexing and unflexing on the steering wheel. Her face is in the dark. I think, Jeez, she's a beautiful woman. Light does funny things.

I say, "Come on back inside. We were just getting started."

She just lets it roll back, and we're out into the street. Lucky I live in a quiet subdivision, because I look like Fool Number One in that sheet. I honestly do not know what to think about women sometimes.

Finally she says, "Well, thanks for the beer," and puts the car in Drive, swings it around.

It made me mad, the way she just said that and pulled away. I hollered after her: "You could at least give me my money's worth."

She stopped. I walked down to her car.

"Just what would give you your money's worth?" she said.

I suggested some things.

She sat there for a minute and I thought, hell, maybe she *is* a whore. Then she said:

"You are a sick son of a bitch."

"And you are a lazy piece of pussy." There we were. The car was still in Drive, its motor was running. Somebody went past but I didn't pay any attention.

She says, "Well. Now that we've introduced ourselves, good-bye."

I try to say something more, but she steps on the gas and she's gone. Too bad. She was a spunky gal and I like a spunky gal. I wish I had her phone number.

Bill Burkens and Peter Krull

It is late. Peter Krull has his lights turned off. He stands at the kitchen window of his upstairs apartment and looks out over the divider fence into his neighbor's yard. Beneath him, Mrs. Townsend, his landlady, has been asleep for at least five hours: Peter heard the bathroom pipes rattle, heard the clunk of the two-by-four she fastens across her door.

His neighbor, Norman, is likewise fast asleep; his light went out a good three hours ago. Norman too is security-minded, though not of the passive beam-across-the-door type. Norman bought a mercury-vapor light and put it on a pole in his back yard. Now the whole neighborhood glows like a shopping center parking lot. But that wasn't enough: Norman bought a German shepherd. The light keeps the dog awake all night. It barks at passing airplanes. It barks at imaginary cats. It barks at Peter, when he sits up at night. So Peter keeps the lights off, a tiptoeing burglar in his own home.

Peter has decided to get drunk tonight, but the process is taking longer than he had counted on. He fingers the ice cube tray on the table beside him; eight cubes left, enough for two drinks plus a half. He holds the bottle up to the green glow of Norman's security light. Trouble. Either just enough or not quite enough. Either he will drink himself into sleepiness and get a few hours' rest before work, or he will drink himself awake and have to call in sick at eight, when the sleepiness finally hits.

"A borderline situation," Peter says. The German shepherd in the yard next door, sharp-eared and not the least bit sleepy, sits up at the end of its chain and whines. Peter makes a face at it, then chuckles at his ghostly green reflection in the window. Norman and his light. Mr. Security.

Peter doesn't like to fall asleep these days; his dreams are bad, and he wakes up tired. He takes catnaps, and if he drinks enough in the evenings, he can usually get two or three hours of rest just before dawn. At the newspaper where he works, he goes to the darkroom in the afternoon and sleeps. His boss no doubt knows this by now, and Peter in turn knows that this year or maybe next year he will be canned.

"This will be a problem," he says. Nervous Norman's nervous dog, his fellow insomniac, hears, and yips tentatively.

Peter opens the window softly and speaks to the dog, his voice barely disturbing the still November air. "Here I am, Bowser. Just me."

The dog starts to bark in full voice now, leaping at the darkness outside its green circle of security. The chain jerks it onto its hind legs as it barks in wild rhythm.

"Just me, boy. Nobody out here to hurt you. This is just Piedmont, Bowser. Just a little town." The dog becomes frantic; after a few minutes, Norman's bedroom light snaps on. Peter slides the window down.

Just a little town. Hardly enough crime to keep the sheriff busy. Or the reporter, for that matter. Peter Krull, soon-to-be-ex-reporter for the *Banner-Press*, knows that as well as anyone. Why not sleep in the darkroom all afternoon? Nothing happening anyway. Peter watches Norman's stairway light come on. In the ell window there is a glimpse, a vision: Norman in bathrobe creeping downstairs, baseball bat in hand. The light at the bottom of the stairs comes on; outside, the dog sits quietly, wagging its tail.

Peter fishes two ice cubes out of the tray and refills his glass. Hard to be a reporter in a town where nothing ever happens. It's enough . . .

Enough to . . .

*   *   *

It had been a Monday when the sheriff called the office. A Monday in late July or maybe in early August. The sheriff's name was Junior. Junior was a big burr-headed cigar smoker with a face that had squinted too long. Over the phone Peter heard him puff his cigar between sentences.

"We got a fella's drowned hisself out by the lake, if you're interested."

"You bet. He still out there?"

"I'm gettin' up a coroner's jury now. Gotta view the scene, you know."

A lousy story. Not worth bothering about, really. But it was already Monday, the *Banner-Press* went to print on Wednesday, and Peter still hadn't found anything to fill the front page. Better a drowned man than nothing. Besides, he could get a photo of old Junior looking official, build up brownie points for the next time something really did happen. So he grabbed a camera and took down Junior's directions.

The location was about twenty minutes west of town. Peter followed the highway until it turned toward the lake; a dirt road continued west. After a few miles, the dirt road forked. The right fork Peter knew; it went through heavy timber, passed a few summer cabins, and eventually returned to the highway. The left fork was hemmed in with multiflora rose on both sides, and a stripe of grass ran down its center. Peter turned left.

The road quickly became a trail of rocks and ruts. Peter drove in first gear. Ahead, he saw the sheriff's patrol car and the coroner's black van parked at a narrow turnoff beside a locked gate.

Junior was leaning against his car, smoking a cigar, in his usual uniform and cowboy boots. The coroner was a middle-aged, egg-headed man named Norris; he had his handkerchief out and was polishing the side insignia on his van: "Norris Funeral Home" in chrome letters above a pair of chrome praying hands. Peter parked his car in the weeds beside the road and got out; a faint odor of death hung in the air.

"This the place?" The two men looked at each other as if there might be doubt that this was the place; then Junior nodded.

"Waitin' on the jury," he said. "Howell took 'em over to get swore in."

They were standing beside an unmarked mailbox. Behind them a lane led through overgrown fields to a little house trailer about eight feet wide, rusty white with a horizontal pink stripe.

"Nice house," Peter said.

Junior laughed. "Just big enough to go crazy in."

"That what's up?"

The sheriff flipped his cigar butt into the road. "Could be."

"You got a name yet?"

Norris flipped through a pocket notepad. "You'll have to hold it until we say so. We're still looking for next of kin. Name's William Burkens, that's k-e-n-s. Middle name none or unknown."

"Anything else?"

"Nah."

Another patrol car came into view. It was crammed with people; Howell Adams, the deputy, was driving. Peter recognized the rest of them as courthouse loafers, most of them retired men, men who started their day in the Kozy Korner, drifted to the courtrooms and public offices about noon, and ended up sipping coffee in the Zephyr Cafe in the interminable evenings.

Howell stopped in the middle of the road and opened the back doors for the old men.

"Six good men," Howell said. "Signed and sworn."

Norris gave them all surgical masks. "Follow me, boys," he said. "Better put those on."

They climbed the gate and walked single file down a cowpath that angled through the field, tying on their masks. But the odor penetrated easily; tears came to Peter's eyes as he blindly followed the sheriff's wide brown back through the underbrush. The path ended at a clearing where the ground dropped off sharply to a pond thirty feet below.

"You boys can stop here," Norris said. He scrambled down the slope on his hands and knees and waded into the pond. William Burkens, middle name none or unknown, was floating a few feet from the bank, swollen as far as his clothes would allow. Norris pulled the body toward the shore by a trouser leg and fitted a heavy rubber bag over it. One of the old men leaned heavily against Peter, as if he had lost his balance; Peter turned to see him stagger, then grope his way back up the path, holding the sleeve of his flannel shirt against his face.

Norris turned the body over and rolled it into the bag. Peter heard the old man off in the weeds and covered his ears so the sound wouldn't get him started. Rising partway from the pond, Norris slid the body into a second bag, then a third, and dragged it onto the bank. He walked slowly up the hillside, shaking mud from his rubber boots.

The group walked back to the cars without speaking and joined the other man, who was sitting in the road with his back against the patrol car's front bumper.

Norris kicked off his boots in the grass, reached into the back of his van, and dug out a squeeze bottle of disinfectant. "I recommend a verdict of death by accidental drowning," he said, scrubbing his hands and arms.

Junior looked around. "All in favor?"

The men raised their hands. "Thanks, boys," Norris said. He touched the deputy's shirtsleeve. "Howell, you want to give me a hand with this?" The two of them pulled a stretcher out of the van and started down the path. Junior lit a cigar.

"Let's go take a look at that trailer." he said.

*   *   *

Outside, Norman has begun to swat at the dog, cursing halfheart-edly: "Sell your ass, that's what I ought to do. Worthless mutt. See how you like the junkyard life." The dog evades the blows, but doesn't cringe, and Norman keeps the baseball bat uplifted in his other hand. The dog bites, after all; the sign on Norman's front yard gate says so. Dog Bites. And while it's reputedly a one-man dog, faith-ful unto death et cetera, Norman doesn't have enough confidence in the Rin-Tin-Tin mythology to storm right in there without the bat. Those two juicy white shanks between the bottom of the robe and the top of the corduroy slippers may prove too inviting, may re-arouse the atavistic wolf-genes that supposedly lie dormant in its dog-soul. The Call of the Leg.

"Don't blame you a bit, Norm," Peter says. "Let him know who's in charge."

The dog hears; Norman does not. Peter can sense its confusion as it hops from side to side in front of its doghouse. To bark or not to bark? Barking is its purpose in life, its very definition: watchdogs watch. Guard dogs guard. But there's Norman, standing over him, drowsily angry. The dog compromises, barks once but conceals it as a yawn. Norman cinches his bathrobe tighter around his waist and retreats, huffy, to his castle. Peter refills his glass.

Here at the upstairs window, he feels ripe, good, capable. He is safe. He can make his observations and his comments freely, give rein to his thoughts.

He moves closer to the window and studies his reflection. A moon-green face lit from beneath, a puffy, soft-edged face that seems perpetually on the verge of acquiring character. The harsh shadows accentuate the sagging circles under his eyes; when he was thirty, he had confidently expected them to make him look Auden-esque. Now Jesus Christ he is thirty-eight, and those droopy circles just make him look beat-up, hung over. It crosses his mind that tomorrow might be a good day to call in sick—a slow day, plenty of time to catch up later. Tomorrow is the day his boss composes his editorials, and he always reads them to Peter, who is thereby forced to put on a serious expression. His boss, James J. McQuay, inherited the *Banner-Press* from his father, Dwight David McQuay. Peter knows that he should rightly feel contempt for him—the contempt one reserves for a fool in a position of authority—but can't summon it up. He regards him as no more than a persistent annoyance, a turned-up nail in his shoe, a tacky commercial, a barking dog. Contempt would require a greater investment of emotion than Peter is willing to allow; so he just avoids the man.

Editorial day, however, stretches Peter's power of forbearance. James J. McQuay sits at his desk across the office from Peter, his brow furrowed, cribbing phrases from the area dailies all morning and most of the afternoon. "Which do you think sounds better, Pete?" he says, poised over his keyboard. "'The people in Europe must think we're made of money' or 'The people in Europe must think we're made *out* of money'?" Peter has to stop and pretend to ponder. "The first one, I think." "Me too. Less wordy." In the end, he types them triumphantly, signing each one "JJMcQ." All This Fuss About Foreign Aid. JJMcQ. Needed: A New Marshall Plan. JJMcQ. What Ever Happened to Respect for the Flag? JJMcQ.

Norman's dog has settled down into the puddle of light in front of its doghouse, resting its chin on crossed paws and gazing up at Peter's window. Now and then one ear will pivot like an independent creature toward some unknown sound.

Tomorrow will be a good day to call in sick. Just stay at home and see what goes by.

The door to the trailer was ajar. Junior took a notepad from his shirt pocket and handed it to Peter. "If they's any valuables, I'm going to take 'em to town and lock 'em up," he said. "You keep a list."

The sheriff stepped inside, his cowboy boots clumping on the thin floor. Peter could hear the distant voices of Norris and the deputy hollering instructions at each other. He followed the sheriff up the trailer's steel mesh steps, ducking under a spiderweb, and paused in the doorway.

Junior stood in the center of the living room. He kicked the sofa hard, and a cloud of dust rose from it. An instant later, a frightened blacksnake thrashed out from under the sofa, writhing in all directions at once, and then spurted for the door. Peter leaped back, surprised and afraid, and tangled himself in the spiderweb he had so carefully avoided the moment before. The snake disappeared under a junked washing machine that sat in the yard.

Junior barely turned his head. "Mice," he said.

The living room was tidy and impersonal. They started with the desk; hung above it was a *Farmers' Almanac* calendar with a circle around a date still two weeks away. On the desk itself, a stack of bank statements, each with *balanced* written neatly across it, sat beside a pad of clean white paper. As they moved, they stirred up more dust in the stale trailer air; Peter began to sneeze, picking cobwebs out of his hair. He leafed through the calendar while Junior opened desk drawers. No more days were circled.

"Looka here," the sheriff said. He flipped through three savings passbooks, one from each Piedmont bank. "Nineteen thousand four hundred. Eleven thousand one hundred. Twenty-four thousand even." He licked his thumb and paged through a checkbook. "They's another two thousand in this 'un."

Peter wiped his nose on his sleeve and walked into the bedroom. The walls of the trailer were just narrow enough that he could stretch out his arms and touch his fingertips to each side. The bed was made, and the clothes were hung neatly in the closet. No photographs on the dresser, no souvenirs stuck in the mirror. The room was as functional and anonymous as a motel.

Pushed to one side of the closet, behind the shirts and jackets, was a spotless, pressed Army uniform in a plastic cleaners' bag. Junior came into the room; he reached over Peter's shoulder and fingered the service ribbons on the jacket.

"Southeast Asia," he said, and turned away.

Peter looked at the uniform a moment longer. On the sleeve were the stripes of a first sergeant; they seemed strangely large, gaudy. He hung it back up.

"Put this on your list," Junior said, rummaging through the chest of drawers. "One Purple Heart."

The sheriff lumbered onto his hands and knees to look under the bed. "Put this down," he said, groping. "One Remington twelve-gauge shotgun, pump action. One .22 rifle, bolt action, uh, Mossberg."

Peter moved back through the living room to the kitchenette at the other end of the trailer. He heard the quiet *snik* of the .22 and the deeper *cha-klok* of the shotgun as Junior checked their chambers.

"Put down 'moldy' by those," Junior called.

The kitchenette was sunnier than the rest of the trailer; the end window, uncurtained, shed two squares of light across a dingy blue Formica table that had, instead of legs, a pipe in the center screwed into a fitting in the floor. A light film of greasy dust covered the table, the sink, the refrigerator, and the two-burner propane stove. Wasps were building a nest in one corner of the window.

"Guess that's it," Junior said, slamming his last drawer. They carried the guns, the bankbooks, and the medal up the lane to the sheriff's car and loaded them in the trunk. Everyone else was gone. Peter helped him string tape across the gate: Police Line. Do Not Cross.

Junior gave him one of his foul cigars, and they sat on the hood of the patrol car and smoked.

"So why do you think he did it?" Peter said.

"Could have been an accident."

"Yeah, but I mean the whole bit. Living out here like a tramp, saving all his money. Doesn't make sense."

Junior shrugged. He blew one smoke ring, then another, and watched them rise and dissipate in the hot, hazy sky. "Maybe he didn't like people," he said at last.

"I figure there's got to be a better reason than that. People don't just sign off."

Junior puckered his lips and flicked an invisible piece of dust from his pants crease. "Maybe so. Couldn't prove it by me."

Peter was insistent. "People have reasons for doing the things they do. Things don't just happen without cause."

Another smoke ring. "Whatever you say, philosopher. I wouldn't know." He stood up, crushing his cigar butt underfoot, and got into his car.

"You really think it was an accident?" Peter called after him.

The sheriff paused with one foot on the ground and one inside the car, unwrapping his next smoke. He bit off the end of his cigar and spit it into the weeds with an explosive sound.

"Pond was only four foot deep," he said, tapping his index finger lightly on the steering wheel.

"But the jury vote? Accidental drowning?"

"What's the difference?" Junior said. "He didn't leave no note. Maybe he was standing up on the bank and had a heart attack." He got the rest of the way into the car but then rolled down the window. "If you don't mind, I'd just as soon you didn't mention all that money in your article. We'd have half the county out here digging up his yard." He rolled the window back up and drove away.

The article! Peter swore at himself. He'd forgotten all about it. Nothing to do now but try to pick up stray threads. He took a photo of the Police Line sign with the trailer in the background: scene of the—of the what? The tragic accident. The mysterious death. He drove back to town trying out headlines: Local Farmer's Death Ruled 'Accidental.' Mysterious Accident Claims Recluse.

At the funeral home, Norris was examining the damp contents of the dead man's wallet. A few loose facts: seventy-one years old. A brother in Lompoc, California, Warren Burkens.

"You notified this guy yet?"

"Oh, yes," Norris said, as if the question was too obvious for serious consideration. "Of course. First thing."

"What did he say?"

"He just said thank you and to contact the VA about burying him. Said to let him know where they put him."

Peter couldn't reach the brother that afternoon, so he came back to the office that night to try again. He doodled on his notepad while the phone burred; a man's voice answered, thin and stringy over the distance.

"Mr. Burkens?"

"Yes?"

"My name is Peter Krull. I'm writing your brother's obituary for the local paper."

"What?"

He raised his voice. "I'm writing your brother's obituary. I'm sorry to disturb you."

"You mean Bill. He was my half-brother."

Peter wrote that down. "Right. Could you give me any background information on him?"

The voice was dull. "I never knew Bill. He had already left home when I was born. I met him a few times. We sent Christmas cards. But other than that—" His voice faded away.

"I understand he was in the Army," Peter called. Sitting at his desk in the darkness, he suddenly felt attenuated, weak, as if the faraway voice was all that kept him from vanishing entirely.

"Yes, that was during Vietnam," the brother said. "He went over there, I think."

"Do you know of anything else I should include in his obituary?"

"No . . . no." There was a pause; the line hummed and crackled. "I suppose you think I haven't been a very good brother. I haven't kept up."

"No," Peter said. "I don't think that at all."

"He wasn't my full brother, you know."

"Yes. Thank you."

Peter pours his final drink, which he now knows will not be enough. Sleeplessness wins tonight. But it will be a good day to call in sick anyway—editorial day, obit day, news release day. Peter has been thinking about his job a lot lately; he feels like a parasite on the miseries of others. He gobbles up their sorrows and spits them back out trivialized. Last week he put two headlines side by side on the front page: Teen's Joyride Ends Tragically. Downtown Merchants Plan Moonlight Madness. And as he swallows his drink, letting its sour sharpness fill the back of his mouth, he realizes that he never wants to go to work again. He would like to stand at his window from now on.

Peter was lucky the week Bill Burkens died. A boiler exploded at the high school, killing the janitor and forcing an evacuation; Peter had some genuine news, some fresh misery, to fill the front page. He didn't have to whip up the Bill Burkens story into something it wasn't, just wrote a standard obit and put the photo on page two with a brief accident report.

But he couldn't let it rest. He told himself it would make a good story, and half believed it. A real think piece. Study of a Loner. Bill Burkens bothered him; the blankness of his image called out for features to be sketched in. He went to see the mail carrier, Eddie Lyle, who had first reported the stacks of catalogues and circulars that were piling up in the listing mailbox. "The pension check, that's what really made me start to wonder," Eddie said.

Peter was treating Eddie to beers at the Country Gentleman; he signaled for two more. "That right?"

"He used to ignore the third-class for days and days, just leave it in the box. But he'd always fish out that pension check right off."

"This was the veteran's pension?"

"Yeah. Department of the Army. Seven hundred a month. Not bad for doing nothing, don't you think?"

"Seven hundred. How do you know?"

"Easy. Window envelopes. You take 'em like this and you squeeze 'em just so, and you can see right down the window."

Eddie drained his glass, his eyes suspicious and appraising. Peter signaled for two more.

"You want to know what I think?" Eddie's voice was getting scrambled. He drummed his knuckles against the edge of the table. "I think there's gotta be something *wrong* with a guy'd live out by 'mself day in, day out. You know? Nothing but Walmart ads and bank statements, that's all I ever took him, them and them checks. And every year a Christmas card. One fucking Christmas card. You want to know what I think, I think maybe there's a little, you know, shell shock. You know?" Eddie tapped the side of his head. "Maybe still hearing them cannons?"

Shell shock. "The very word is like a bell," Peter says, and crunches his last ice cube. Norman's dog hears him again and tries a quiet growly bark—just enough to ward off an intruder without waking up the household.

Calling in sick, of course, will set off the standard murmur, secretary to business manager, business manager to JJMcQ, everyone to everyone: Krull called in sick again. JJMcQ will frown thoughtfully for a moment before returning to his newest creation, Drugs: The Hidden Menace. Peter will sleep, awaken, sleep, awaken. Then comes evening, and zip goes Peter down to the Country Gentleman for a quick beer before coming home to think. Peter needs a lot of time to think these days.

After Eddie, Peter tried Ben Boatwright, the American Legion commander. "Sure I knew him," Ben Boatwright said, his voice the rolling growl of a worn-out transmission. "We give him a flag ceremony up at the cemetery. He was a vet, you know."

They sat at a table in the Legion Hall. Two men were playing pool; another hung streamers from the rafters, red and blue, with cardboard leaves and shocks of corn.

"So what did you know about him?"

"I know he liked to be left alone. I ast him to march with us in the horse show parade one time, him being a vet and all. He just said no thanks."

"What else did he say?"

"Nothing." Ben Boatwright croaked out a laugh. "I guess I don't know too much after all. You coming to our Labor Day dance? Bill Brown and the Mountaineers."

Peter rose to leave and shook his hand. "Might be able to. I'll have to see."

Ben Boatwright gripped him by the shoulders and leaned into his ear; the tattoos on his biceps were blurry and sagging. "You know what I hear? I hear he was wounded, you know. Had one of them steel plates in his head."

"Thanks," Peter said, and left.

Nothing, nothing, nothing. Nobody knew anything. The real Bill Burkens, whoever he was, was missing in action. Peter felt irrationally angry at this man he had never met, this vanishing man, who had no reason for doing any of the things he did, no reason at all.

He drove from the Legion Hall out to Bill Burkens' trailer; it was early September, a humid, sluggish day. The sheriff's line was still up; the gate was still locked. So was the door, but he kicked it in easily, one good hard blow, and crashed into the musty interior.

It wasn't mice after all that had brought that blacksnake inside, it was eggs, her own eggs, and they had hatched, two dozen tiny blacksnakes squirming across the floor, toward, then away from, the sudden light, then in every which direction like a living carpet.

Peter felt one crush under his foot as he paced the tiny trailer, looking for—

Looking for what he hardly knew. He felt himself treading the boundary between curiosity and illness and didn't care. People's lives had to make sense. This man's life had to make sense. Otherwise—otherwise he couldn't imagine.

The explanation, the clue, had to be here. He had just missed it the first time, or seen it and failed to recognize it. He shuffled through the papers, the calendar; he jerked the sweat-stained shirts from their rack in the closet and threw them onto the bed. He ripped the cleaner's bag off the old Army uniform. A baby black-snake crawled up his pants leg; he shook it out with an impatient stamp of his foot.

He paced until evening fell, feeling his way along the walls, ruffling and ruffling the stacks of paper, sitting in the broken-down easy chair to watch the snakes race back and forth across the living room floor. When it got too dark to see, he gathered up some of Bill Burkens' belongings and drove slowly home.

Dawn breaks. The security light switches itself off; the dog falls asleep. Peter goes into his bedroom and sits on the neatly made bed, thinking.

He thinks about the pursuit of security, how security imprisons at the same time that it frees. He believes now that he understands Bill Burkens, has come to admire him, even love him. The only truly harmless man he ever knew, the only truly secure, truly free man. Just exercising his freedom; it is so simple, so sensible.

He digs through the box of things he took from the trailer. They're all that's left of Bill Burkens now; the sheriff sold everything else at auction and sent the money, after probate, to the brother. Bill Burkens has almost disappeared altogether.

It's nearly time to call in sick. He fishes out one of Bill Burkens' old shirts, a faded cotton plaid, and tries it on. It buttons up easily, and Peter watches himself in the mirror. He holds out his arms. It almost fits.

Magic Kids

The change in the sound was almost imperceptible, with the radio playing and the traffic noise, but somehow they all knew from the disappearance of that one note—the baritone hum that they could never even have said they heard—that they had run out of gas.

Dad was at the wheel and instantly at the edge of something, crying or shouting or what, couldn't tell yet. Mom sat in the passenger seat with her arms folded. She was always at the edge of crying so being at the edge of crying was nothing new. In the back seat, Will didn't much care. Being out of gas was just as interesting as having gas.

"I knew we should have got gas at that last place," Mom said. Dad hit the wheel with the heel of his hand. Nobody wanted to mention that the last place, Warsaw or Clinton or wherever, was where they had changed drivers, and she could have filled up the car just as easily as anybody. Besides, miracles abounding, the exit ramp was a down slope and Dad, hauling against the dead power steering, got them to the light and managed to switch with Mom while the light was red, shoving against the back of the car while she steered, and this place being almost like the country, far enough west of Kansas City to feel like something more or less rural, people jumped out to help him push and within a minute they were in a station and miracles abounding, the hotel was just across the way.

Dad was again at the edge of something, although now it was joy or singing or whatever, his clothes dirty as they checked in but his face filled with a smile at the kindness of strangers. Magic Kids had gotten them a suite, so Will had sort of a room of his own, at least with its own TV set, which was cool. Dad took a shower while

Mom called Magic Kids to let them know they had arrived. Will wanted to check out the TV, but first there was the round of pills.

"Am I going to have to come in there and remind you to take your pills?" Mom said. Will was already halfway done.

"No," he mumbled through a mouthful. Will didn't mind the pills. They just took practice.

Then there was time for PlayStation. Dad and Mom stayed in their room and made phone calls, called Grandma and uncles and aunts, called the radio stations and the TV stations, the people back home who had raised money. Everything looked good for tomorrow. The weatherman said it was going to be a nice day. He spoke in hard, flat syllables as though his voice were bouncing off a metal roof; Will had never heard anything like it, even though Kansas City wasn't all that far from Mountain View. Will wondered whether the guy was making it up, but Mom said they all talked that way up here.

"There's no plug-in for my clock," Mom said. "Dennis, find a plug-in."

"There's a clock here."

She gave him her look. "You know how I hate those cheap clock alarms. That nasty buzzy sound. Scares me to death. Besides, they don't work half the time. You want to sleep through this?"

Will didn't feel much like eating that night. Everybody thought he was too excited, and he let them think that. Truth was he was having a bad day.

The lady from Magic Kids came over later. She was a sharp-faced woman with dyed black hair, and she didn't look at Will with that moony expression so many people took on. Will liked her for that.

"How old are you, young man?"

"Fourteen."

She sized him up. Of course he was small for his age. All his food, all his energy, had been going to The Thing for years.

"I think you'll fit in the seat okay. You realize," she said, turning to his parents, "that there is risk involved anytime you step onto a racetrack." His father nodded, almost too eager. "You'll need to sign some releases. After you're done at the track, I have some passes for the National Agricultural Hall of Fame, if you like." She laid them on the side table and glanced at Will, whose face must have revealed something. "It's very interesting."

Will watched while they went through the paperwork. Finally, it was over.

"You a big NASCAR fan?" the woman said.

Will nodded. "Yes, ma'am."

It wasn't true. The races on TV bored him, but his dad liked them, and they were a good way to spend time with his dad in a way that didn't end up in shouting or crying. When they got approved by Magic Kids, he figured what the heck, nothing else he really wanted to do. Dad would get a kick out of being in the pit area.

Another round of pills, and Will lay on his bed watching TV with the sound down while Mom and Dad slept. He could feel his insides working. Maybe it was just his imagination, but it seemed like as soon as he got sick he became able to feel what was going on in all his internal organs—his stomach, his kidneys. He could feel his heart working, not just the beats, but all the separate movements of the muscle. He felt fluids running in and out of his liver.

Will put on his clothes and slipped out the door, blinking in the unexpectedly bright light of the hallway. He could see two doors open at the far end and heard the sound of voices—kids his age, it sounded like, on a field trip or something. He thought about going down to say hi, but didn't. With his bald head and wasted face he'd just freak them out.

He ended up at the vending machines by the front desk. The desk clerk was a stout woman, maybe thirty-five, with bobbed brown hair and a pair of thick glasses.

"You need anything, honey?" she said.

"No, ma'am," Will said. He'd forgotten to put any change in his pants, so there was no point in standing at the vending machine. Nowhere else to stand, though.

"You here for the Kansas Speedway?"

"Yes, ma'am. I'm—" Not much to say. He let it run out.

"We get three or four of you fellas a year," she said. "No girls. Guess they all want to go to Disney World or somewhere."

"Guess so."

Will walked to the door. The parking lot was quiet. The highway seemed empty, although he could see headlights and taillights tracing its path.

"What you going to do there?"

He turned back to the desk. "One of the drivers said he was going to take me on a few laps."

"Which one?

"Mark Sharp."

"Oh, honey, he's cute! Wish he'd take me on a few laps."

"That's my dad's favorite driver."

The woman was rustling papers, clicking her computer mouse, tearing sheets off the printer from time to time. She perched on a padded stool, giving Will an occasional glance.

"You say you get a lot of kids like me?"

"Mmm, like I said, four or five. Our chain is a national partner with Magic Kids," she said, with a momentary note of pride in her voice. "Some of 'em come in, they are in ba-ad shape. One little boy, couldn't hardly even talk. He was in a wheelchair, kinda leaned over all the time." She seemed about to say more, but then thought better of it. From a mount in the far corner of the room, a shopping channel danced silently. "Now you, you look pretty good."

"Yes, ma'am, I feel okay." And it was true. Whatever it was that had kept him awake had gone for now. "You got any kids?"

Her face seemed to open and then shut. "One, but he has passed away. He had a heart defect. Passed away at two and a half months."

"Oh. I'm sorry."

"Thank you."

For a couple of minutes their silence was broken only by the clicking of her mouse. The woman lowered her eyes to her computer screen and Will, embarrassed, leaned against the front desk and looked out the door. He'd known this silence himself. Friends would come by, his friends, his parents' friends, and they would accidentally say something painful. And then the silence, or worse, the rush of apologies, more words trying to cover the earlier words, but never succeeding.

He looked back over his shoulder at her. Her name tag read "Ruby Simmons."

"Mrs. Simmons?"

She looked up, her face composed.

"I'm very sorry about your son," Will said.

"Thank you again." She smiled. "It was ten years ago next month."

"What was his name."

"Aaron. His daddy and I picked it out together."

"That's a good name."

Ruby Simmons turned back to her work, and Will thought he should probably quit talking. He felt sleepy.

His father woke him in the morning dressed in his Mark Sharp jacket complete with advertiser patches. Mom was already down in the breakfast room.

"At least somebody got some sleep," she said to him when they brought their trays. "I don't see how you do it. Your father and I tossed and turned all night."

Soon the Magic Kids lady was there, shiny in black and red polyester, and they were checking in at the speedway. A knot of people waited at an entrance.

"We're from Mr. Sharp's team," someone said. "And you must be William."

Then before he knew it they were standing at the edge of the racetrack, patting themselves in the crisp air, one of the team off apart with her back turned, talking on a cell phone. A black car gleamed nearby.

"He's not going to stand us up, is he?" Mom said. "It's three hundred miles."

Someone had a souvenir Mark Sharp jacket for Will, and he put it on, grateful for the warmth. And then there he was, the celebrity, striding out from a door Will had not noticed before, big smile, fast walker.

Dad made a strange noise like a moo. Then they all began to talk at once.

Mark Sharp was a small man, wiry and muscular, not much taller than Will himself. In their jackets, Will felt as if he and his dad were badly drawn cartoon versions of the real Mark Sharp, who stood relaxed, letting the effusions of his parents wash over him. At a pause in the talking, he stepped over to Will.

"So what do you say, buddy? Ready to roll?" And poof, they were in the car.

"Now this is not my real car, you understand," Mark Sharp said. "My real car, you have to climb in the window. This here's the pace car. But you know that."

He eased the car though the first few gears. "So how fast does your dad drive?"

"I don't know, eighty maybe on the interstate."

Mark Sharp smiled a practiced smile. "Okay, here's eighty."

Scenery flew past, advertising signs, fences, people. As they made a curve, invisible hands pressed him into his seat.

"Now here's a hundred," Mark Sharp said. "Now ten."

Will knew he should respond—whoop, or yell, or something—but he just felt content to watch it all go past.

"This is twenty."

Will watched his parents flash by. They seemed to be clapping or waving.

"You ever worry about getting killed out here?" Will said after a while.

"God, yes. All the time. Can't let it mess you up, of course, but still. Especially nowadays, with some of these new drivers they've let in. Bunch of ignorant motherfuckers—" He shot Will a glance. "Oops. Sorry about that. We're supposed to watch our mouths, too. No more cursing."

"It's okay."

"You should hear me after the races. 'Well, gosh darn it, if it hadn't a been for that doggone tire going out on me on 42, I would been in the doggone top ten.'"

They shared a laugh, and then Will said, "Listen, would you mind giving my dad a few turns around the track? He's the real racing fan of us two. He's been wanting to come up here for the Richard Petty Driving Experience, but we never could afford it."

Another glance. "Okay, sure. Just as well. They throttle you down on that Driving Experience. Hell, more thrills on the L.A. Freeway than that thing." He poked Will in the side, gently, with the knuckle of his index finger. "Now if you see Mr. Petty, don't tell him I said that."

They rolled to a stop by the knot of people. Mom was clapping her hands and Dad was making big windmill motions with both arms.

"How about you, poppa? Want to take a turn?" Mark Sharp said.

"Um, the release forms—" began one of the assistants, but the driver cut her off.

"Heck with the release forms, we're just gonna take a turn. Test out this new asphalt they put on. Come on, what do you say?"

And he and Dad were off, sweeping through the curves like before. Mark Sharp was probably saying "Here's eighty." They flashed past, his dad a blur of waving hands. Will thought he heard a whoop.

The air had begun to warm up. Will was about to unzip his jacket when he caught his mother looking at him out of the corner of her eye. She would just make him zip it up again. The small talk had trailed off, and they stood quiet, the sound of the car faint as it sped down the backstretch.

"You get all the cars in here on race day, and it is loud, loud, loud," the assistant said. "But you know."

"No," Mom said. "Never been to a race. Meant to, but with Will—" She stopped herself, and the silence returned.

After a couple more rounds, the car pulled to a stop again and the men got out. Dad had a look of goofy pleasure on his face like a drunk. They all shook hands again, standing in a small circle, and Mark Sharp's crew returned to their cell phones and stepped off to the side.

"So you heading back home?" Mark Sharp said.

"Yes," Mom said. "Tomorrow. Tonight we'll have a nice dinner and rest."

"So buddy, what you gonna do once you get back home?" Mark Sharp gave his shoulder a soft punch.

"I don't know," Will said. "Die, I guess."

In the silence that suddenly deepened and surrounded them, silence that reached all the way out into space, Will could feel the others rearranging themselves, reallocating their positions in the small circle they had formed at the edge of the pavement, an edge, he noticed looking down for the first time, that was cracked and invaded by tendrils of crabgrass and chickweed. Will didn't know whether to take that as a sign of hope or one of disheartenment, the stubborn persistence of life or the inevitable victory of chaos. He could feel his body at work, its ceaseless labor, blood flowing in and out of The Thing, his nerves firing, electrons jumping from synapse to synapse.

"Well, fuck," Mark Sharp said.

"My beautiful son," said Mom.

And then the moment was past, they all talked at once again, just as at the beginning, covering as best they could the embarrassing truth. Mark Sharp jumped to join his crew, who were ready with new sheets of paper, new public relations events. They disappeared as fast as they had arrived. Mom and Dad and Will stood on the concrete apron of the track, aware of the Magic Kids lady waiting for them at the gate and the National Agricultural Hall of Fame in the near distance. But none of them moved to leave, not quite yet.

Late and Soon

Chester's father had gotten him the job, although no one mentioned it. He had muttered gruffly, the way a person speaks when he is about to embark on an indirection, that he had heard from his golf partner, the property manager, that there was an opening in sales, and Chester was sensitive enough to the rules of gruff mutterings to pick up the overtones.

It was Chester's weekly Sunday dinner with his parents, and they stood in their customary places on the deck, his father at the railing watching the golf carts hum up the valley, Chester against the wall watching his father. It was seven o'clock; the midsummer heat still lingered; but his father liked to stand on the deck in the evening, being manly, ignoring mosquitoes.

From the kitchen his mother cried: "A job right here in Belle Prospect! Wouldn't that be convenient?"

"Oh, convenient, for sure," Chester said. He didn't know why his mother's quivering, hopeful statements always brought out a sarcastic tone. But they did.

"I don't mean convenient for *us*, I mean convenient for *you*," she said as a smile rushed across her face on its way somewhere else. "You wouldn't have to move. And——" She wagged her finger at him, and this time the smile was completely fake. "You could get married to Maryalice, with a steady job."

"She's already got a steady job."

"You know what I mean, young man. She may put up with this living-together business for a while. But take it from me, you can't keep a good woman waiting too long."

A number of different replies, all of them querulous, occurred to Chester, who said nothing.

His father said: "Let's not get the cart before the horse. He hasn't even gotten the job yet. When he goes for his interview, the thing to avoid most of all is acting sullen. That's the one trait an employer can't stand, and I speak from experience here."

Chester turned away, sullen despite himself, and contemplated his universe. Below, the deep valley, hardly wide enough to hold the winding golf course that ran through it. Between the house and the golf course, a rocky hillside, thickly forested with oaks and hickories. At night raccoons came out of the woods and scuttered across the yard onto the deck, looking for scraps. Chester's little house barely visible at the far corner of the acreage, where in the nights he could hear the whir of the treadmill and the clank of the weight machine from his father's basement gym. Then the yard, weirdly bright from fertilizer and constant watering, where his father sought to hold back the disorder of nature with a 48-inch cut, zero turning radius John Deere. Inside, tidy suburb: fireplace, gleaming wood, many television channels. On the mantel were a brass retirement plaque from the company, some golf trophies, and, in a frame, his father's combat medal.

That night he had Maryalice cut his hair. He sat in a kitchen chair, a towel around his neck. She was a big woman, tall and strong, wide in the rear, her arms and face deeply tanned from her job as a flagger for the highway department. Everyone in Belle Prospect had a tan for one reason or another, except Chester, who spent too much of his time in bars.

"You want to keep the ponytail?" she said. The kitchen scissors were dull; they pulled.

He shook his head. "I told him I'd go to the interview. I might as well do the rest." She unwound the rubber band at the back of his head. "It was just a little stub anyway."

"Do you want to go, or do you just want to make your dad happy?"

"I'd rather have him happy than unhappy. And the money would be nice." The scissors creaked. She lifted his chin with her free hand.

"Money," she said. "I thought we had money figured out."

"We do. It's not the money."

"Then what?"

Chester felt his mind going into idle, his nobody-home-here mode, where it stayed most of the time out in the real world but which he usually avoided in the cabin. He knew it annoyed Mary-alice, and he didn't want to annoy her. He forced his mind back.

"Maybe it is my dad. Maybe it's worth it, on the off chance that it will make him happy. I've spent plenty of time making him unhappy. What do you think?"

She wet a comb and pulled it across the top of his head. "Getting thin up here."

He waited as she snipped and combed, her hip warm against his side. No need to repeat his question; she always answered in time, always in the same way, sympathetic but cutting no corners on the truth. No excuses. She played fair. That was what had drawn him to her in the first place, what had led him to invite her to the cabin he had built in the scruffiest corner of his father's double lot.

"Your dad's thing is pride. He wants a son to be proud of. Pride is not your thing. It's a cheap satisfaction. The question is, can this job at the land company give your dad his thing without taking away your thing. I think probably not."

She stood back for a moment to check the evenness of the cut. "On the other hand," she said, "maybe it can and there's only one way to find out. How do you like your new look?"

Chester took the mirror from her hand. Before, he had looked like an aging hippie, soft from too much beer, partly bald, strings of gray in his red beard. Now he looked like an aging hippie with a haircut. They looked at each other, knowing this, and smiled.

Maryalice said, "Somehow I never imagined you in sales."

* * *

The sales manager said: "Heard you might be coming by. Welcome aboard. My name's Dale Green." Dale Green grinned cheerfully, but his look said jeez-another-loser.

There was no interview. The job had been wired, golf partner to golf partner: his father, mayor of Belle Prospect, and what's-his-name, the real estate hog. Dale Green handed Chester a three-ring binder stuffed with bullet lists and simple graphs.

"Here's the deal. People come down here for two reasons. A, they want to retire and play golf, like your dad. Those are the easy sales. You show them the course, drive them around for a couple of hours, bring them back here to the sales room. Half the time you don't even have to put in the DVD and go through the flip book. Just give them a contract and off you go."

Chester opened the ring binder to its first page, a plat map of the Belle Prospect development. Down the center ran the creek, once upon a time Sulfur Branch but now Belle Prospect Brook, and along the creek was the golf course. It ran the length of the map, the holes laid out end to end so that hundreds of lots could touch or overlook it.

"B, they've gotten our brochure or responded to the cold call. Free weekend at the lodge if they agree to hear the sales pitch. Those are the hard sales. They think they're going to get something for nothing. Your job is to make sure they don't. Come over here."

Dale Green walked to the back deck of the real estate office, which like everyone's deck overlooked the golf course. They watched the carts navigate in slow procession, up one side of the creek, down the other. "Selling things is an art," Dale Green said. "It is also a war. How old are you?"

Chester had been lulled by the flow of words. He jumped. "Forty-three."

"I'm forty. Were you in the military? Desert Storm maybe?"

"No."

"College?"

"For a while."

These answers did not appear to satisfy Dale Green. He returned his attention to the bright green swath below, shimmering in the summer heat. "I was in Afghanistan," he said. "The thing nobody understands about war is how hard you have to think. Out there is your enemy. He wants something from you. You want something from him. You have to think, think, think, all the time. Your life is at stake."

He smiled, a blissful wide smile. "Here it's just the same, only you count money, not bodies. Every sale is a battle, and don't you forget that. When somebody arrives for their free weekend, you say to yourself: 'Those people are carrying a seven-thousand-dollar commission in their pockets. That is my commission. That is my money. And if they leave without buying a lot, they are taking *my* seven thousand dollars away with them.'"

Below, a foursome had stopped their carts in the fairway and gathered in a nervous, foot-shuffling ring. They thrashed with their clubs at something in the middle. Copperheads were still a problem in Belle Prospect.

Dale Green took Chester's elbow. "If I was walking out this door with seven thousand dollars of yours, wouldn't you want to stop me?"

"Sure."

"Wouldn't you find some way to stop me?"

"I guess."

"Wouldn't you *make sure* I didn't leave with your money? Grab me by the arm? Take hold of my lapels? Persuade my wife not to let me leave? Wear me down, talk me to death, until the only thing I wanted was for you to let me go, until I would gladly, cheerfully, give you your money, if only you would let me go?"

"Well—"

Dale Green had him by both elbows now. Chester could smell his breath, a mixture of cigarettes and mints. "That's what you have to do, Chester. They may hate you later, as they drive home. They have just bought a vacation lot they will never use. They wish they had been tougher. They wish they had never heard of Belle Prospect. But when they walk in this door, they are carrying your paycheck. You have to make them give it to you. You married?"

"Ah, no."

"Girlfriend?"

"Sure."

"Well, just wait till you're like me, a married fellow with three little cuties, and some bastard is heading out of here with my commission still in his pocket. You say to yourself, 'There go my kiddies' Christmas presents,' and brother, you want to let the air out of his tires. Anything to keep him here for another dose of the sell. You got any nicer shirts than that? Never mind. You will soon. Now settle down in an office and look over the material."

Chester spent the morning studying the book, which he was supposed to flip through, page by page, as he delivered the pitch. After the plat map came a series of graphs, all heading dramatically upward: real estate values, number of people owning second homes, tax benefits, something called the "comfort living index." Each page was encased in heavy plastic. There was something reassuring about the laminated pages, so shiny and permanent, with their forceful yet modest messages of hope and prosperity.

Just before noon a maroon SUV pulled into the parking lot. Dale Green watched them stretch their legs, a young couple with a little girl. "Ugh," he said. "Hyundai. Only cheapskates drive Hyundais. What the hell, Chester, you gotta learn sometime. They're yours."

Chester practiced his salesman's faces as he walked out to greet them—hearty eagerness, amused hauteur, bluff honesty. He settled on bluff honesty, feeling their suspicion play over him like a steady breeze. Their names were Jack and Deanne, and the little one was Kal. "With a K," Kal said. He checked them into the lodge, and they arranged the sales tour for five o'clock.

"Well?" Dale Green said. "Where they from?"

"Kansas City."

"Whereabouts in Kansas City? What do they do for a living?"

"I don't know."

"Know your enemy, Chester, it's the first rule. How many suitcases they bring?"

"Well—"

"I know, you didn't notice. Listen, little things mean a lot. More suitcases, the more they like possessions. Good sign. Whoever fills out the guestbook is the one who had the idea to come here."

"It was the man."

"Attaboy. You'll make a salesman yet. Any bumper stickers? Check for them, you can learn volumes. No bumper stickers, bad sign. Means they don't tell people what they're thinking." He gave Chester's elbow a squeeze and left for lunch. There were no bumper stickers on his car.

Chester picked them up in the company car, an elephantine white Lincoln. "Money likes money," Dale Green had said, explaining the extravagance. "Money is like a starling. It likes to congregate with other money. You want to make people feel rich."

"I want you to know right off the bat that we really don't have any intention of buying a lot down here," Jack said as soon as they were in the car. His voice was nervous. "You look like the kind of fellow who would understand. I mean, you people send out thousands of those flyers, you've surely got to assume that a certain percentage of the people just won't be interested. If you have something better to do with these two hours than talking to some people who are definitely uninterested—you know, making phone contacts or doing paperwork—"

Deanne spoke from the back seat, where she was trying to get Kal involved in a finger game. "I'm sure this gentleman has to take us on the tour regardless. After all, we agreed. It was right there on the form."

Chester remembered Dale Green's words and found to his surprise that he was already thinking of these people as an enemy. The cash nexus, the money thing, had hold of his brain. He hated them.

"I don't have to take you around Belle Prospect," he said. He felt a grin wrap itself around the lower half of his face, wider and wider, beatific, maniacal, a Dale Green smile. "It says that in the ads, but no one will check up on us. We could go spend two hours in the movies and no one would be the wiser."

He started the car.

"The reason I'm taking you on the tour is that I love this place. I think it has all the right elements for a fine young couple such as you. Plus signs all down the list. When you got out of your car this afternoon, I said to my boss, 'There is a Belle Prospect couple.' I specifically asked to be your sales guide. And once you understand Belle Prospect the way I understand Belle Prospect, you'll love it too."

His grin would not leave. He put the Lincoln in drive.

Rhapsodies came to him, salesman's poetry. He drove them down the east side of the development, stopping at all six scenic overlooks. He stopped in the Village Square, waved in the direction of the Town Hall, bought Kal a sundae at the Kreem Shoppe. The temperature sign on the Village Bank said ninety-six. He drove back up the west side; five scenic overlooks.

"Next we take a ride in a golf cart—right down the middle of the most beautiful golf course in mid-America. You play golf, Jack?"

"No." Jack was looking fatigued.

"How about you?"

Deanne met his eyes in the rearview mirror. "Golf?" she said. "Christ."

"That ice cream was gross," Kal said.

Once in the cart, Chester tried another tack. "What's your line of work, Jack?"

"I'm in marketing, and Deanne does public relations. She's quite—"

"And neither of you plays golf? A little advice, kids. Where do the real decisions get made? On the golf course! A mid-level manager who can't talk golf might as well say, 'Don't move me up—I'm happy where I am.' And think about saying to your boss, 'Come on down to our woods place this weekend. The house is small, but you won't believe the golf.' What an impression!"

Chester steered the humming cart down the hot asphalt path. Jack and Deanne were silent. They passed his father, whacking savagely from the rough, and Chester waved.

"Village mayor. Lives next door to me. Fine fellow."

His father straightened and waved, then returned to his practice swings. Was there pride in that wave? Would there be another set of gruff mutterings on the green, indirections made with eyes averted—*that your boy up there?*—the kind of man-talk that meant so much to the old bastard? And why should that matter to Chester?

On impulse he swung the cart around. "We've got time!" he cried. "Let's say hello. That's the terrific thing about this development. Your neighbors are your friends. You make friends so fast!"

"Are you sure you know how to drive this thing?" Kal called from the back.

Chester felt burdens lifting from him as he approached. Perhaps he could make his father happy; what would be wrong with that? Who had been expecting too much from whom?

"Jack and Deanne, meet Ben Wilson, our Lord Mayor. And the little one here is Kal." His father looked the part, tanned and firm, like a model for a line of senior citizens' sportswear. His creased smile, his perpetual squint, looked newly handsome to Chester. They were on the same side at last. Hands were shaken all around.

"Having a good stay?" When his father asked the question, suddenly Chester could see in the couple's grim, polite smiles and tight nods that nothing was right. They saw him for a phony, they hated the tour, they weren't going to buy a lot. His father's squint darted his way: appraisal, judgment, confirmation, disappointment. Chester knew he never should have tried.

"Your name is Wilson too, isn't it?" Jack said.

"That's something, eh?" Chester said. "And we're next-door neighbors."

"They better rename the town," Jack said. His father merely looked from one face to another, silent.

The conversation ran on cruise control for another minute, then a foursome arrived at the tee behind them. His father tried to give him a questioning look as they parted, but by then Chester was deep into nobody-home mode.

It had always been that way, Chester thought. The unspoken comment, the dubious look. Success loves success, money loves money—Dale Green was right about that. But he forgot the B-side of the song: money hates no-money, success hates no-success. Or is embarrassed by it, which is worse than hate sometimes.

At least he could punish these Starbucks drinkers. At the end of the golf course was a chair lift that took them back to the lodge. "You'll love this part," he told the little girl. "You can see for miles."

"Rides make me sick," she said.

"How much more of this fucking junk do we have to listen to?" Deanne burst out. "It's hot as hell. I could have been laying out, or better yet home in my air-conditioned house, and here I am riding in a golf cart. I hate golf. This ski-lift thing doesn't even look safe."

"Your vulgarity surprises me, ma'am," Chester said. "But to answer your question, you have—" He showed her his watch. "—twenty-two more minutes of me, and then you are free. And if you don't like the lift, the steps are over there. Know what a copperhead looks like? Never mind," he said, as they all jumped into the lift chairs.

At the office, he gave Kal a lollipop and took them onto the scorching deck with the flip book. The child appropriated the only shady corner, staring moodily into space and sucking loudly on the lollipop. Chester opened the book to the map page, his voice oratorical, pitched to reach Dale Green, who was spying from behind a partition.

"From where we stand, we can see fourteen lots that are still unsold. These are prime lots, highest value in Belle Prospect, and of the fourteen, twelve directly overlook the golf course. Frankly, I can't understand why they haven't been snatched up already. Looking south down Belle Prospect Brook, we can see two lots remaining on the east side, near Village Square, and on the west side more than—"

At the corner of the deck, Kal began to vomit. The air was filled with the sick sweet smell, ice cream and illness, and Chester had an instant recollection of his own childhood, when he always got carsick from reading comic books and had to be let out on the roadside, his father standing impatiently above him while his mother cleaned his face. Deanne ran to her and carried her inside, followed by the men.

She glared at him. "You got a towel?" Chester looked around wildly, as if a towel might have nestled unnoticed among the framed photos and piles of brochures. He gave her his handkerchief. Deanne wet it in the water fountain and bathed the girl's face.

"Okay. Happy now?" she said. "Well?"

Chester said nothing.

Soon Kal was back to normal, and the family stalked out. Chester watched them return to the lodge, unconsciously folding and refolding his fouled handkerchief. He became aware of Dale Green behind him.

"I don't think this is my line," Chester said over his shoulder.

Dale Green's face was averted. "Bring back the goddam Lincoln before you leave."

In the golf cart once again, Chester passed beneath his parents' house. A thought struck him: it was past six—what the hell, she'd be home. He turned the cart off the path and drove it up the hill on the winding service road, the puny battery straining under the labor. He pulled into the driveway and took the turnoff to his cabin.

Maryalice was sitting on the porch. She cocked her head as he drove up. He didn't get out of the golf cart.

"I forgot to tell you something my mother said the other night."

"Okay."

"She thinks that we ought to think about starting to talk about maybe getting married."

Maryalice smiled.

"Oh, she does, does she?"

Unexplained Aerial Phenomena

Janine had ended up teaching at Dower College by accident, more or less. She was from St. Louis and had never been to Springfield, as far as she could remember. Her family oriented east: one set of grandparents in Baltimore, another set in Philly, and cousins all up and down the seaboard. Her schooling had followed the same path, and although she had never been as intellectual as some of her classmates, she had done well for herself. DePauw, then Ohio, and finally Pitt—none top-tier, but all entirely respectable. But when it came time to hit the job market, her advisor reminded her that the harsh laws of supply and demand applied in the academic world as much as anywhere else and that first jobs were not the place to get picky. The supply of sociologists, alas, outstripped demand by a considerable factor.

So when she applied to Dower, she played the Missouri card as hard as she dared, and apparently it worked enough to get her an interview. After that, who knows? Somebody liked her. Maybe the other candidates were awful. Didn't matter, she had the job.

The dean was a little fellow with an English degree from Arkansas and a sly way of implying that people weren't working hard enough, even during praise, and her department chair, Mr. Hardin, was a holdover from ancient days, with only a master's degree from Northeast Missouri State, which wasn't even Northeast Missouri State anymore. In her first month in Springfield, the chair had invited her for dinner at his home, where they labored at conversation over roast chicken. Mr. Hardin and his wife were pleasant people, wrapped up in college politics and their distant offspring; Janine delicately fished for clues about how to get ahead at Dower but received only murmurs about collegiality and good evaluations. Mrs. Hardin offered to fix her up with some fine young men of her acquaintance, the nephews of friends and people from her church, but then stopped herself.

"Unless you're—uh—"

As a grad student, Janine might have enjoyed discomfiting an oldster navigating the new intricacies of gender, but she was not a grad student any longer, and besides she liked to think she would have better manners than that anyway. So she tapped Mrs. Hardin's arm and said, "This year is all about establishing myself profession-ally. Next year, I'll turn to my love life."

Mrs. Hardin looked relieved, and Mr. Hardin cleared his throat approvingly.

Over the next few months, she settled into her apartment and job and looked for a research project. The dean could rhapsodize all day about the joys of working with undergraduates, but Janine knew that the path upward was paved with publications, lots of them, and in the best journals she could manage. There was only so much dissertation farming a person could do.

"Research something local," Mr. Hardin told her. "We don't have funds to send you to Timbuktu. We're a teaching institution."

Janine had written on theories of crowd behavior. She searched the local news for cases: mobs, hysterias, calamities, follies and delusions. And there it was, a little town to the east, where every-one—or at least it seemed like everyone—had seen UFOs one summer a couple of years ago. Perfect.

She spent a few weeks reading until she felt ready to drive out for a look on an October afternoon when she had no classes. Pine Hill looked like every other town she had seen during her time here: aging, piss-pot poor, Trumpy beyond imagining. A Corps of Engineers lake outside of town, over which the mysterious lights had hovered. A Casey's and a Dollar General, a hamburger place, a consolidated school district, a bank branch. In the bank branch would sit a branch manager, whose children would one day be sent to Dower College to be bleached of their small-town ideas and sent off to law school, and with any luck they would return only for reunions and retirements.

Janine found the newspaper office. The editor, a middle-aged man in a button-down shirt, studied her for a while before speaking, which left Janine acutely conscious of her out-of-place looks: her oversized black sweater with a showy scarf to look dressy, her exaggerated eyeglasses, her unkempt hair. Of course outsiders would be resented. But what could she do? She was who she was.

"We're a pretty conservative town here," the editor finally said. "Not like you folks in Springfield. The TV people came in and kinda had some fun with us, so don't be surprised if nobody wants to talk to you."

"I'm not a TV person. I'm a scholar."

"We had some of them too. Didn't act much different, if you ask me." He consulted his computer and wrote an address on a slip of paper. "Woodrow Bird lives out by the lake. He's the first one who saw them. He still talks to everybody. Other than that—" He shrugged. "This UFO thing is the first time Pine Hill's been in the news since the fireworks factory blew up. Nobody likes to be a laughingstock. Don't expect much cooperation."

The joys of field work. No wonder she had preferred theory in school. She typed the address into her map app: the highway heading east, then a squiggly line, then a squigglier line.

Woodrow Bird sat on his front porch as Janine's car pulled into his circle drive, looking like the stereotype come to life. He looked to be about seventy-five, square and solid as a cinder block, with gray hair cropped so closely that it might as well have been shaved. He wore a pair of Big Smith overalls that had been with him for quite a while, and, to complete the postcard, a dog sat beside him. He listened gravely as Janine introduced herself, then stood to shake hands.

"Janine," he said. "There's a fine old-fashioned name."

"It was my aunt's."

"That's a good tradition, not that anybody ever asked me. Family names are the best names." He sighed. "So you're here to talk about the flying saucers or whatnot."

"Yes."

"UAP, that's what they call them now. Unexplained Aerial Phenomena. Guess 'UFO' had too much of a woo-woo sound for people. Anyway, come on in."

Woodrow Bird's living room was tidy and minimal, old pine flooring and rag rugs, with a free-standing woodstove near one wall and a couple of worn couches with throw blankets tossed over their backs. He led her through it to a room behind, wide and narrow with a wall of windows that looked out over the lake.

"This was my wife's sewing room before she passed away," he said. "Since then I've been using it as a catchall."

A jumble of fishing rods and tackle boxes stood by the back door. Against the inner wall were a couple of easy chairs, facing outward, with a round glass table between them. Woodrow gestured toward them, and they sat down.

"Here's where I sit of an evening, enjoying the sunset with my friend Jim."

"Jim?"

"Beam." He chuckled at his well-worn joke. "So here's where I sit, and on the evening in question I was looking out over the lake like usual, and then here come this light from off thataway."

He pointed to his right. Whatever else might be said about Woodrow Bird's house, Janine had to admit it had a fine view. The shoreline was a hundred feet away, down a gentle slope, with no houses visible on either side. Across the lake, she could see the distant shapes of buildings.

Woodrow followed her gaze. "Everybody wants to live over on that side to be close to the boat dock and the café," he said. "Me, I figure if I wanted to clump up with people I'd just stay in town."

"That makes sense."

"So. Here comes this light, and I figure it for a helicopter because of how it moves. Then I think, helicopters make a lot of noise, and I don't hear a thing, so now I'm guessing it's one of those drones people are flying nowadays. So I watch it, and it comes my way, getting bigger. And it's too big for a drone." Woodrow stood up, gesturing dramatically toward the lake. His story seemed over-rehearsed, but who was Janine to say? Even the rehearsed could be true.

"And then——" He took a beat. "The light went down in the water. I could see it going down below the surface."

"How do you know? It must have been dark."

"Oh, it was dark, surely. But at a certain point, when a light is so far below the horizon, there's only one conclusion."

Janine wasn't so sure, but she wasn't there to chase the story anyway. Her goal was to trace the information pathways, the ways in which the story spread, mutated, sank, and resurfaced. Its truth didn't matter, or at least didn't matter much.

"So then what happened?"

"I watched for a while. Seemed like it was coming this direction, right into my cove." He pointed below them.

"Did the light get bigger as it drew close?" She couldn't help herself. She wanted to hear the whole implausible tale.

He gave her a glance out of the corner of his eye. "Not as much as you might think. I believe it was either a running light, or the craft went deeper as it got closer. Then the light went out, just snap, like you flipped a switch."

"Then what did you do?"

"Watched for a while to see if it come on again. When it didn't, I called my friends Lowell and Mike, and they came for a look. These are real people, not like my joke from earlier."

Now she was getting somewhere. Janine drew two circles on her notepad and connected them to a circle in the middle. Woodrow, then Lowell and Mike. The network began. "And then the TV people?"

Woodrow laughed. "Nah, they came on their own. Lowell and Mike came out, and we poked around with our flashlights down at the shore. Couldn't see nothing. So that's when we called the sheriff's department to see if they knew anything." He shrugged. "And then the fun began."

"Pretty crazy, was it?"

"You could call it that. Channel Three, Channel Ten, then the St. Louis stations, then the national shows. It was a nuthouse, especially after all those other people started reporting lights."

"Do you think they're telling the truth?"

"I was telling the truth. Why wouldn't they be?" He sat back down in his chair and looked out at the water. "I tell you one thing. If I'd a known all the grief I was going to get for seeing it, I'd a kept my mouth shut. And to think, I always wanted to live near water."

Janine found herself unexpectedly sympathetic to this man, whom she had imagined from the news stories to be some kind of boastful attention-seeker. "So the sheriff called the TV stations, or they picked it up on their scanners."

"I don't think so. It wasn't till the state trooper saw the lights a couple of nights later that the media people showed up."

The afternoon slanted toward evening. The slope from the house to the lake was a patchwork of post oaks and cedars, filtering the light as the sun dropped over the water. At the edge of the yard, a home-built boat dock extended twenty feet into the lake, with a stubby bass boat tied up at the end of it.

"There'll be a fine sunset in another hour," Woodrow said.

"I can see why you moved out here." But of course there was work to do, so she returned to her chart. Woodrow in the middle, then branches to his two friends and to the sheriff's office. A new circle—she labeled it "media" for now—with a question mark beside it and a dotted line to the sheriff. She riffled through her notes. "I read a news report about that trooper, but he seems to have dropped out of the scene pretty quickly."

"Yeah." Woodrow heaved himself to his feet and walked to the living room door. "They shut him up in a hurry. Said he was bringing discredit to the force." He stepped inside the living room, returning in a moment with a large three-ring binder. "I kept a scrapbook if you want to look at it."

"Of course!" Janine took it from his hands. Page after plastic-sheathed page of clippings, photographs, webpage printouts. This would save her hours of work. "Could I borrow this for a few days?"

"Don't see why not, as long as you bring it back. I only look at it now and then."

"I promise." A week to photocopy, cross-reference, and map, and she'd have her rumor transmission model all set. Apply some theory, and boom: conference paper, journal article, book chapter.

"You look like I just handed you the Scripture."

"Mr. Bird, you have no idea. Nobody indexes these little publications, and it would take me ages to run down all these stories, their dates, who's quoted, who spoke to whom—" She made a helpless gesture. "This scrapbook solves most of that problem. Is it up to date?"

Woodrow shrugged. "Pretty much. Maybe not the last few months."

Janine imagined this man, hunched over his newspaper with scissors and rubber cement, printing off news stories from television websites on his fifty-dollar inkjet, memorializing this one great anomaly in his life. "I'll take good care of this."

She flipped another few pages, and a photo caught her eye: Woodrow and someone else in these very chairs. "Is that William Shatner?"

"That's him, all right. He was only here for half an hour, just long enough to tape his introduction. Some kind of unexplained mysteries show. Nice fellow, very pleasant."

Janine sat in William Shatner's chair and pondered the strangeness of it all. A small town, a quiet lake, and then a year's worth of media madness and celebrity. And now obscurity in the wake of that upheaval. Scrapbooks and where-are-they-now articles. She stood up.

"I've taken enough of your time," she said. "Can I bring this back in a couple of weeks?"

Woodrow walked her to her car. "I'll tell you another thing," he said, pointing to the scrapbook on the seat beside her. "If you're looking for the truth about those lights, you won't find it in there."

"The story matters as much to me as the facts. How it spreads, what kind of needs it meets." Seeing his skeptical look, she added, "Every story fills a need. Why does a station run a story about mysterious lights in the air above Pine Hill instead of a story about something else? That's what I'm curious about."

Woodrow seemed unconvinced. "Well, if you ever decide you want to get closer to the truth, let me know." And as she put her car in Drive, he added casually, as he turned toward his house, "I still see them pretty regular."

Back at Dower College, Janine's semester foundered. Students openly checked their phones during class, wandered in and out of the room, turned in sloppy or plagiarized assignments. "First-semester shakedown cruise," Mr. Hardin said. "Don't worry about it." But the dean furiously scribbled notes during his visit and e-mailed her articles on classroom management.

Mr. Hardin chuckled as she described her research. "I remember that business. Biggest thing to happen in Pine Hill since——"

"Since the fireworks plant exploded."

"Pretty much. Anyway. Talk to Psychology and Communication. Maybe we can put together a symposium. Think your source might be willing to appear on a panel?"

Suddenly Janine felt protective of Woodrow Bird and his eccentric scrapbook. Her research was one thing, but a public event, with random curiosity-seekers and equally random but incurious students, seemed invasive and inappropriate. "I don't know. I think he's been burned before."

"Can't hurt to ask," he said, and Janine took that as an instruction.

But first she needed to think. She mapped out Woodrow's scrapbook, the spread of stories from local to regional to national, the details left out or blurred along the way, the transformation into familiar tropes. Just as Woodrow had said, a highway patrolman reported the lights three days after Woodrow, only to waffle and then grow silent a few days later, when the TV crews appeared.

Woodrow's parting words echoed in her mind. He hadn't sounded like he was joking, but the news stories never mentioned any such claim. And why tell her, of all people?

She called him one evening under the pretext of setting a day to return his scrapbook. But her question could not be restrained.

"Woodrow, when I was leaving, you told me that you still saw these UFOs."

"UAPs."

"Right, UAPs. Were you just teasing me? Or is that the truth?"

"Miss, do I look like a chronic liar to you?"

"No."

"There you go then. Come on out if you want to try to see them too. Tuesday nights are the best. I only see them at night, and for some reason they like Tuesdays. Dress warm, 'cause we have to go out on the lake."

Janine drove out to Pine Hill the following Tuesday with a mild sense of apprehension. She didn't particularly like the outdoors, although she enjoyed a walk in the park once in a while. But a boat on a lake, even on a calm fall day such as this one, fell outside her comfort range.

*   *   *

Two pickup trucks were already parked in Woodrow's driveway when she pulled in, and two more old men standing in the yard.

"Welcome to the Senior Center Boys' Club," Woodrow said. "This is Lowell and Mike."

Lowell was a tall man, only slightly stooped, with a shiny head of silver hair that he combed straight back, the kind of man who would have been thought handsome in an earlier day, and he still had the air of someone who took care with his appearance. Mike was bald, short, and chunky, with a gray goatee and a checkered fleece coat spotted with oil stains.

"So he's roped you into this shit now, has he?" Mike said.

Janine didn't know what to say in response, so she simply followed them into the house in silence. Woodrow had spread out a map of the lake on his kitchen table. He placed the saltshaker on a spot midway up the eastern shore.

"Here's us. What I've seen, the things seem to like to come and go from this cove just to our north, around the point." He traced the path with his finger.

"The things," Lowell said.

"The little green men," said Mike.

Woodrow looked across the table at Janine. "You see why I never went back to the news people. Even my own friends give me shit."

"Aw, we love you, Woodrow," Mike said. "We're here to help you welcome our new alien masters."

Woodrow did not take the bait. "This bluff along here is the old jumping-off bluff. Before they built the lake, it was a deep hole of water where the kids would prove their courage by how far up they would climb before they jumped. Deepest place in the lake except up by the dam."

"Lowell wouldn't know about that," Mike added. "He's a newcomer."

"Fifteen years," said Lowell.

"You're a newcomer until you have two generations in the cemetery," Mike replied.

"Focus, boys," Woodrow said. "We need to get in motion. Here's what we'll do. Mike and I will take one boat and ride out to the far end of the bluff, drop anchor, and wait. Lowell and Janine, you'll take Lowell's boat and go to the near side, just past the point. If we see anything, we'll take pictures and hopefully catch it from two angles. If we haven't seen something by nine, we come back and make toddies."

"You're just a regular General Patton, aren't you?" said Mike.

Woodrow didn't answer, but led them to a large Rubbermaid storage box just outside the back door. He pulled out four life-jackets and handed them around. "We're not taking any chances out there. No arguments."

No one argued as they walked to the boat dock, where a second boat was tied, a little cruiser with some storage space and a windshield. Mike poked her in the ribs. "Lucky girl. You get the good one. Woodrow and me are going to freeze our asses off in that bass boat."

"So why are you coming?" she asked him.

"Are you kidding? I wouldn't miss this for the world."

Lowell climbed into his boat and helped her in. They let the other two pull away first, then cast off their ropes and followed into the growing darkness.

Woodrow's dock light disappeared as they rounded the head-land toward the jumping-off bluff, leaving only the distant glow of the marina settlement across the lake to their left and the receding glimmer of Woodrow's running light ahead of them as signs of human presence. Lowell proceeded at an idle, the boat motor rumbling beneath their deck.

"Is this safe?" Janine asked.

Lowell pondered. "Yes and no," he said after a while. "Calm night, nobody else on the lake, and if somebody comes toward us we'll see them a mile away. On the other hand, we're on a lake in the dark. It's cold, there could be floating debris, and if you fall in I'm not sure I could pull you back over the side by myself."

If Lowell had further thoughts, he didn't add them. The boat putted along until it reached what Janine could only assume was the predetermined spot, where he cut the motor and tossed out a small anchor.

"I'm not much of a conversationalist," he said. "Mike knows how to keep up a patter, but I don't. I'm sorry about that."

"That's all right," said Janine. They settled into the silence as the sound of Woodrow's boat faded.

The slightest of breezes chilled her cheeks; she cinched the lifejacket tighter over her coat and pulled her knit hat over her ears. As her eyes adjusted to the darkness, more and more stars appeared, stars upon stars, spilling across the sky as if from a knocked-over bucket.

"There's something I never saw in St. Louis," she murmured.

Lowell chuckled. "That's the very thing I said my first night here."

"You're from St. Louis too?" She fought back the impulse to ask what high school he had gone to.

"Yes, ma'am. Born and raised, lived and worked. Bought a cabin down here, which is how I got the idea to retire here after my working days were over. I wanted the peace and quiet. I know that's a cliché, but thirty years at the GM plant is an education in the value of peace and quiet." He drummed his fingers lightly on the steering wheel of the cruiser. "And the loneliness. Now that's part's crazy, but after all those years of work, and the neighborhood, and the church, and the kids and grandkids, I wanted to get used to the feeling of being alone. I figured either me or my wife would need to practice the skill of living on our own. It takes practice, you know." The surface of the lake rippled ever so slightly as the breeze picked up. "Turns out it was me."

Janine wanted to ask more but held back. The moment seemed delicate, and she didn't want to delve any further into Lowell's thoughts than he was willing to go on his own. She thought of her own loneliness, which felt so intense these days, the loneliness of being in a new place with uncertain expectations and doubt as to whether she could meet them. How pale, how puny, her loneliness was compared to his, for as painful as it was, somewhere inside she had faith that it would someday be relieved. But Lowell's certainty was the precise opposite, and she had a hard time imagining how it could be borne.

"Grand Valley," Lowell said.

"What?"

"That's what they called this place before the lake was built. You can see the old photos down at the Historical Society. There was a little settlement, maybe a dozen houses, with a school and a church and a cemetery. The Corps relocated the graveyard, but everything else—"

He gestured out over the water.

"You don't think that had something to do with—?"

Lowell scoffed. "I'm a silly old man, Miss, but I don't amuse myself with ghost stories. I leave the theories to Woodrow."

Janine didn't answer. The conversation disoriented her. Here they sat, rocking gently on the ink-black water with the speckled sky above, and she felt overcome by an eerie sensation that they were not merely floating on a lake, but floating in space, untethered and beyond all reach. What was she to make of all these things? Drowned villages and flying saucers.

Lowell's phone screen glowed green in his shirt pocket. He took it out and studied the message. "Woodrow thinks he saw something," he said. "Only it's not up in the sky, it's under the water."

"What's that supposed to mean?"

"Heck if I know. He just said, 'It's moving along the lakebed.'"

They each looked over their side of the boat, Lowell on the left, Janine on the right. But she saw only scattered glints on the surface, the random noise of the universe, returning nothing meaningful to her gaze beyond the darting glimmers of starlight.

But then she saw it, and from his grunt she knew that Lowell saw it too. Ahead, deep under the water, a green glow moved toward them with the speed of a fish but steadily and on a straight line. It was too deep to make out clearly: a running light, an emanation, a ghost train? Who could know.

It passed under their craft without so much as a ripple, and they scrambled to the stern to see if it came into view again. And in a moment it appeared, receding at that same swift and steady pace, until in the middle distance it vanished as if suddenly switched off, just as Woodrow had said. The whole event happened so fast that Janine doubted herself for a moment. But of course she couldn't doubt it, she'd seen it, as plain as the nose on your face, as her mother used to say. Or as plain as an underwater glow could ever be.

"Don't guess you took a picture with your phone," Lowell said.

An absurd question, for no picture she could have taken would have looked like anything other than a smudge. Janine didn't answer, and Lowell appeared to recognize that too, for he didn't repeat it. After a few minutes he started the engine and winched up the anchor. "Might as well head in. I think we've seen our last out here."

He steered the boat in at a near-idle, watchful over his headlight for floating logs, until they reached Woodrow's dock. They could hear the putt-putt of the bass boat in the distance behind them and see its light. Janine paused on the dock, but Lowell headed toward the house. "It'll take them another five minutes to get here. Let's warm up." She followed him up the slope.

Inside, Lowell took four tumblers out of a cabinet and placed them on the counter. He poured a half inch of Jim Beam into each and dropped in two cubes of ice. Two of the tumblers went into Woodrow's freezer compartment; he placed one on the table beside Janine and took the other for himself.

"I should have asked if you wanted one," he said. "It's kind of our tradition after an outing."

"Oh, I want one."

In truth, she wasn't much for hard liquor, not since freshman year, anyway. But tonight the sour heat of the whiskey was what she needed. She held each sip in her mouth for a moment before swallowing.

The other two arrived soon and joined them in the back room with their drinks, looking out into the night toward the lake. "What are we going to call it?" Mike blurted. "I'm thinking the Grand Valley Light, 'cause it was right over where the old village was."

"You've got to be kidding," Lowell said.

"What? You didn't see it?"

"Of course we saw it. Damndest thing, too. But I'm not going out and giving it a name. People already have us halfway to the mental home, and I'd just as soon not complete the trip."

Mike turned to Woodrow. "That what you think? You were as excited as I was."

Woodrow shrugged, uncomfortable. "I would have liked to get a better look, maybe a picture."

"Tell you what," Lowell said. "Let's each go home and write down what we saw, best as we can remember. Then tomorrow we'll meet at the coffee shop and compare. We'll see if we have anything to go on."

All nodded, and they turned to Janine. "Can you join us?" Woodrow asked.

The whiskey had settled into Janine's cheeks. She was enjoying its warmth and didn't particularly feel like talking. "No. I have class in the morning."

"Oh, right," Woodrow said. "A working person is among us."

Within a few minutes, Mike and Lowell had excused themselves, with promises of the morning meeting and warm farewells
to Janine. She shook Lowell's hand particularly firmly, for he had
revealed things about himself out on the lake that she suspected he
hadn't even told his friends.

But she didn't join their exodus to the driveway. She had a
finger's-width of Jim Beam left in her glass, and she wasn't ready
to leave quite yet. She swirled the ice cubes in her glass as Woodrow
returned to his chair.

"What do you think?" he said.

"I'm processing."

Of course the three of them could be playing an elaborate joke
on her, to be revealed at some later date when they all needed a
laugh, or perhaps never. Or perhaps someone was playing a joke on
them all, like those crop-circle people of years ago, who bam-
boozled half of Britain with little more than some simple tools and
the people's will to believe. And she knew the literature on mass
hysteria.

But what if she had seen what it had seemed to be, and she had
glimpsed the incomprehensible? What was she to make of that?

Janine did not feel equipped for this thought. She imagined
stepping in front of her Introduction to Sociology class tomorrow
and telling them that she had seen the Unexplained Aerial Phenomenon, or Aquatic Phenomenon in this instance. Their concealed
expressions, their sideways glances. And word would get back to
Mr. Hardin, naturally, and then she'd be an official crazy lady, the
faculty member who went out into the hills and came back spouting
nonsense.

She glanced at Woodrow, who was studying her. "This is quite
a challenge," she said.

"Now that's some fine Ozark understatement. You'll be one of
us yet."

"I thought it took two generations in the cemetery."

"We'll make an exception in your case."

"That's all right. I don't think I fit in here."

"Oh, you fit in just fine."

She appreciated his words even as she doubted them. Hers was the generation of rootless professionals who never fit in anywhere nor needed to fit in, for whom geography was an antique concept, chasing their resumes from Springfield to San Francisco to God knows where. Long-forgotten children jumping off long-lost bluffs into long-gone swimming holes: It was hard to see where someone like her would fit in such a landscape.

"So what did we just see?" she said.

"I don't know," said Woodrow. "But I reckon we just saw the back side of it, whatever it was. And maybe it's best just to see the back side instead of looking face to face. Like Moses in the cleft of the rock."

"Maybe so." And who knows, perhaps she was like Moses sitting here, unaware that her face was shining until her frightened countrymen called out to her. And although she knew it was time to go, she lingered, fitting in for just a little while, sitting in William Shatner's chair while deer rustled in the obscurity outside.

Signs and Wonders

The morning fog from the river came up the hollow slow, and it was slow to burn away. Larry and the other men walked through the wet grass to tend the livestock while the women cooked bacon and eggs in the big skillets someone had borrowed from a church camp. Unidentifiable birds sang. Larry had never been around livestock—in the old world he had managed the produce department at the Shop 'n' Save—so he drew shovel duty, as they called it, avoiding any rough language. They worked quietly in the wet air. It was time to butcher another steer; the men who knew what they were doing picked one out and drove it into the holding chute. At the crack of the .22, Larry barely looked up from his work. The birds paused and then continued.

Larry didn't mind shovel duty. The labor had a quiet mindfulness to it, work as prayer; it gave him the right attitude. The idea in these days was to be low to the ground.

When the morning chores were done, they filed back to camp, or what passed for a camp: a hodgepodge of tents and trailers clustered around a large open-air shelter, which served as cafeteria and meetinghouse. Brother Moore's tent was at one end of the shelter; as they walked by they could see him through the open flap, sitting at a card table, scribbling in a notebook, ignoring their presence, his heavy body hunched over his Scofield Reference Bible. Even at that hour he wore a white shirt and black tie; Brother Moore insisted on appearances.

Today was September 17. The Rapture was two days late, by Brother Moore's calculations. Still, there was no cause for worry. Brother Moore had worked it all out. America's war with Babylon. The Jews of the world assembling. The great power of the north dissolving in strife. True, there could be a few days' leeway—no man knows the day nor the hour—but the signs were in order.

Leatha handed him his plate at breakfast with her special smile. They would have their hour to walk in the pasture after cleanup.

The Rapture gave a deliciousness to everything. What if this bite of bacon were to be his last on earth? Or this bite? What if this cloud, passing overhead just now, were the one to part with a blast of trumpets to reveal Christ descending? Every day glittered with anticipatory bliss.

In the pasture, Larry and Leatha walked in slow loops, careful not to touch. Only a fool would lapse into carnality now. In the center of the field the children of the camp had set up their playground; they chattered and cried in their sharp high voices like a flock of blackbirds.

"The days are warm for this time of year," she said. Leatha was about his age, a plain woman, her skin raw and scrubbed, teeth crooked, a hard, angular jaw, but her manner was gentle. In the old world she had been an aide at the nursing home. Her last name was Good, and the badmouths in church liked to whisper that she traded on that; but to Larry it was an apt coincidence. When the Spirit came over the congregation, she was often the first to feel it. Larry would watch: her eyes, closed in expectation, would open wide with delight, gazing at a spot halfway to the ceiling or perhaps above the ceiling. Her stiff form would sway like a windblown sapling as the waves of revelatory truth swept over her, flowing out of her mouth in transmuted form, unearthly phrases, words that could explain everything if only he understood them. Those were the moments when he loved her, or perhaps loved the perfection that he could cherish but not imagine himself possessing. In transport, she became beautiful, and he told himself that it was the spirit in her that he loved, though he knew there was a tangled thread of lust running through it all.

They turned a corner in the field. Warm for this time of year, she had said. "Makes it hard to cook, I guess."

"Oh, no. We do fine."

They walked on. It was important to avoid negative thinking, which could lead to doubt, which could lead to sin. Still, the Rapture was two days late. Everyone had left their calendars behind; who needs calendars in heaven? But everyone knew.

"Brother Moore looks so tired these days," she said.

"He has a lot to think about." Was that getting too close? What was he trying to say? "Caring for all of us is such a task," he added, trying not to sound hasty.

"It's a blessing we have him." Leatha said. That was a good recovery.

Larry didn't know what to think about Leatha now. Before the revelation came to Brother Moore, they had been keeping steady company, and Larry had been working up the nerve to ask her to marry him. But now he didn't know. Once he had gone to Brother Moore to get his advice, but whenever day-to-day things came up, Brother Moore's face would cloud over with a look of bursting impatience. Larry had just muttered something and left, embarrassed.

After the walk it was time for morning prayer service. Larry and Leatha sat together, a comical sight he was sure, fading singles, the two homeliest people in camp, made all the more comical by the fact that this was the state they would be in for all eternity. In Heaven they neither marry nor are given in marriage, that much he knew.

He drifted into inattentiveness and had to keep pulling himself back to the text: Matthew 25, parables and prophecies. Behold, the bridegroom cometh. The tiny print blurred as he shuffled the pages of his Bible. Larry wondered how it would feel to be a bridegroom, with virgins coming out, lamps ablaze, to lead him inside. Foolish virgins off buying oil. Shut the door in their faces.

The parable led him back to Leatha. Despite himself he imagined her as the bride, shuttered away in a back room of the house, tucked into bed in a crisp cotton nightie. The bridegroom steps in, the room all lit with candles, the door closes with a click behind him. In the flickering light all the marks of care and age, hard work and poor life, disappear.

Larry stopped himself before his mind moved to the next part of the scene. This was bad thinking. His task was to empty his heart, not fill it with sin.

After the prayer service was an hour for quiet repentance. As they all headed for their tents and campers, Brother Moore materialized beside Larry and touched his arm. He tilted his head; Larry followed him into his tent. They sat at his card table.

Brother Moore's huge neck and arms strained against his thin cotton shirt, and he gave off a stale odor, as though he had been stored somewhere for many years. Inside the old canvas tent, where the air too was stale, the odor was magnified. The thick lenses on Brother Moore's black-rimmed glasses enlarged his eyes, which seemed to take up half his head. His flattop haircut was so short that there didn't appear to be any hair at all on the sides of his head, from which jutted a pair of perfectly round ears, absurdly small like the ears of a hippopotamus.

"I have a mission for you, Brother," Brother Moore said. Every syllable Brother Moore spoke throbbed with significance. His voice was breathy and surprisingly soft.

Brother Moore tore a sheet from his notepad.

"I am told certain vegetable provisions are low." He paused, searching Larry's face with his big eyes, which seemed to penetrate Larry's thoughts without revealing anything in return. Of course they were low on vegetables. Why lug out extra potatoes when the end of the world is upon you? But that was more negative thinking. Larry kept still.

Brother Moore returned to his notes. "You're our expert in that department. Deal honestly and get good value. There are still plenty of snap beans on hand, but we need potatoes, cabbage, and carrots. With twenty families, we've been using fifty pounds of potatoes, fifteen heads of cabbage, and ten pounds of carrots per day. So go into Piedmont and buy—" again the pause, the appraising look—"no more than two hundred pounds of potatoes and a like amount of the other items. Use your judgment. Get good value."

Four days' worth. Brother Moore lowered himself onto his hands and knees and fished a shoebox from under his cot. Barely glancing into it he grabbed a handful of money out of the box and handed it to Larry.

"Two more things. Buy candy for the children. And buy a copy of the *Banner-Press* and the Poplar Bluff daily. I want to look for signs. Put those items in a sack and bring them directly to me."

Larry waited until he had walked far enough up the hollow toward the cars to be out of sight, then stopped and counted the money. Most of the bills were twenties and fifties. Larry stopped counting when he passed a thousand.

As he walked, he watched for snakes. Just yesterday, one of the brothers had killed a copperhead, a disgusting fat snake that, headless, still coiled and twisted and seemed to strike, as if the bloody neck could harm. "Just reflexes," the brother had said, spattered, holding the snake high above a circle of children. Larry had never liked the outdoors; he didn't see the fun in living among snakes and bugs. He had borrowed his tent from the meat manager, an avid hunter and fisherman, as he supposed was only natural for a meat manager.

Thoughts of the meat manager brought a pang of guilt to Larry. Most of the people in camp had quit their jobs to come out here, but Larry had just taken his two weeks' vacation. Was that a sign of doubt? He hoped not. Nothing to do now but push it from his mind.

144 / SCATTERED LIGHTS

The cars were where they'd left them, lined up in the old logging road that led into the hollow. They'd left the keys in them as a sign that they were renouncing the world, but the world did not seem to have noticed yet; they were all still there. Larry climbed in the one at the end of the line—Brother Parker's old green Impala—and backed the quarter mile to the county road.

The highway to town seemed unfamiliar. How strange to see people still out there, humming, working, unaware of the catastrophe that awaited. People sitting on their porches, people driving their cars, people mowing their grass! How could they? Larry felt invisible to them, though they waved as he passed. How pretty the houses looked in the sunlight, all the different colors of paint and siding and roofing. Who could have guessed there were so many different colors of roofing? Every house had something different in its front yard, flower beds, concrete deer, birdhouses hanging from the trees. He knew heaven was going to be more delightful than anything he could imagine, but he could not help wondering if he would miss this world, so messy and inventive.

The otherworldly sensation deepened as he reached town and pulled in behind the Shop 'n' Save. He felt like someone back from the dead, wincing at the noise of car doors. He looked down at his hands and flexed his fingers. Nothing looked different, but he thought he could feel the Spirit hovering above him, the way one can feel an electric line close overhead. His soul felt empty, ready, waiting for something to pour through it.

He went in through the back. Inside the store, he waved faintly at the assistant produce manager, laboring over the displays at the far end of the section, too busy to talk, which suited Larry just fine, since he was an unrepentant sinner and a poor judge of vegetables to boot. Larry carried his items outside and put them in the trunk, waiting. Everything had a watery look about it as though it were all going to vanish in another moment. He watched his fingers pick up a pad and pencil, write down the list of items, and sign his name, or a name that seemed to be his. On the way to the checkout lanes, he picked up a bag of candy and the two newspapers. He smiled at the checker, ignoring her idle chatter. He felt sure that if he opened his mouth to speak, out would come unknown tongues, words to amaze, his voice the sound of many waters. But he chose not to open his mouth. Whenever the moment came, it would come of its own accord.

He stepped into the sunlight, walked to the car, tossed the newspapers into the back. But he felt so light, so free, that he couldn't bring himself to get in just yet. He crossed the parking lot and headed down Main Street.

The store windows were full of brightly colored things. Before he knew it he had walked into Randolph's clothing store. He plunged his hand into a rack of winter jackets and pulled one out. It was an M, just his size. Nothing was coincidental. He tried the sport coats along the wall. A nice gray 38S jumped into his hand. He pulled some bills from his pocket and paid the salesman, who hadn't even gotten the chance to greet him.

A tune came into his head as he stepped onto the sidewalk, some old hymn that he couldn't quite place. Where next? He crossed the street to the dimestore and bought a toaster oven.

It was hard to walk carrying the coats and the oven, so he set them down by a light pole. If they were here when he came back so be it. The newspaper office was right there, so he bought a tape dispenser and a box of file folders to add to the pile.

Larry walked a half dozen blocks, turning corners left and right by whim, until he reached the city limits. The sidewalk became a weedy footpath. He paused in the bright sun and looked around. An auto body shop, a row of self-storage buildings, a bar, a rundown motel. And, of course, the church.

He supposed he had been coming here all along. He crossed the highway and walked up the steps.

They had met in living rooms and basements, but when the Adventists built their new church out toward the lake this building had been available cheap. Its windows rattled and it needed a new coat of paint. They had chosen to leave it that way, avoiding ostentation of furnishings. The early Christians met in tombs.

The door, naturally, was unlocked. Larry walked up the center aisle, lightly touching the pews one by one, till he came to his usual place about halfway to the front on the left side. The church had a churchy smell, cool and musty, the smell of hymnbooks and unused space.

Suddenly an old woman rose up out of a pew three rows in front of him where she had been lying—sleeping? She wore an overcoat and a sock cap. Her eyes were encased in puffy bags and her skin was the color of a toadstool.

"I'll be going," she said in a voice that seemed creaky from disuse. She fumbled under the pew.

Larry opened and closed his mouth a couple of times. Finally he managed, "No. It's all right."

"No, I'll be going." The old woman continued to fumble. She seemed to be packing. Larry moved closer—silly to worry about theft, he thought, what's to steal—and saw that she was stuffing an old quilt into a trash bag.

"Really," he said. "You can stay."

"You the preacher?"

"No."

"I'll be going." She swung her feet down and brushed off the pew with a knotty gray hand. "Maybe okay with you, but the preachers they got their own ideas."

"Really. You can stay here as long as you like. We're not going to be using this building. We're—"

It was hard to explain, maybe impossible. The old woman looked at him suspiciously.

"I got a sister in Marble Hill," she said. "Would have rode the bus like always, except they took out the bus anymore. But walking ain't bad."

She glared at Larry, as if daring him to reciprocate. "Everybody in our church is camped down at the river," he said. "We decided—that is, we had a revelation—"

He couldn't say it. It was ridiculous. We think the world is coming to an end. We're all going to be carried off into Heaven.

Larry turned and left, walking fast, not wanting to hear any more, say any more. As he reached the door, he felt the lump of money in his pocket; paused. He peeled off the top bill, a twenty, and put it on the small table by the door.

"Here you go," he said. "This'll get you a ride to Marble Hill, I bet."

He stepped out before she had time to reply. In the parking lot the sun hurt his eyes; he closed them and walked on, gravel crunching under his shoes; bumped into the sign post and leaned his cheek against it, feeling the rough rust scrape against his face.

The post was cool but the air was hot. The spirit was gone. The town looked ordinary. Ordinary cars whipped past, blowing ordinary dust over him.

He made it back to his car after a while and drove to his house trailer. Inside the trailer he filled the bathtub with warm water and got in. He lay there for a long time, idly soaping and rinsing the same leg, the same arm, over and over, until the water was gray and cold. Then he went to the couch and fell asleep.

Larry woke just as the sun was setting. There was nothing to do, he supposed, but drive back to camp. Luckily, he had parked in the shade, so the vegetables weren't spoiled, but most of the candy was melted inside its wrappers. Tough luck.

He took the long way back to the camp, a route that let him drive past Leatha's house. It was a mile north of town on the main road, a small white frame house that she had inherited from her parents, now long dead. Larry stopped the car in her driveway and got out, though he left the motor running. He walked up to her front porch; it was a good porch, wide and shady, with a swing. For a few minutes he sat on the swing and tried to conjure the invisible presence of Leatha beside him, the quiet, commonplace things they would say to each other in the evenings. Sitting out there for everyone to see made him feel conspicuous, and soon he returned to the car, though something made him stay there, looking at the house, for a while longer.

As he walked down the hollow, nervous in the evening shadows, jumping back from tree roots, he smelled the camp before he could see it: wood smoke, cow manure. But when he arrived, Larry realized that the entire place was silent and empty. He peered into the 55-gallon drums that they had cut open on one side to use as cooking pots; the fires under them still burned, the water boiled, but there was no food in them.

This was it. The Rapture had come, and he had been left behind.

An image came into his head—himself, squatting in the empty camp, pouring dust and ashes on his head—and for a moment he thought he would do it. But it seemed too theatrical. Then he heard Brother Moore's voice down by the river.

Everyone was standing on the bank, where the flat ground began to slope. From the back of the crowd, Larry couldn't see; beside him was a redbud tree, forked near the bottom, so he put one foot in the fork and slid out onto the arching trunk.

Brother Moore was knee-deep in the water below them. He had the shoebox of money in his right hand, and in his left hand he held a fat copperhead about two feet long. The snake wrapped and unwrapped around his arm, moving its head from side to side as if seeking a hole in the air to escape into. In the fading light Brother Moore's enormous head seemed larger than ever, but Larry couldn't tell if it were just a trick of the light and perspective. He had never seen him from above.

" . . . like this," Brother Moore was saying. "I strolled in the evening, as is my wont, asking for a sign, in the meadow above the camp. And as I stroll I feel a sting. And lo! This old fellow, this old adversary, lies beneath my heel." He shook the copperhead at the crowd; the snake paused in its bobbing to bite him on the bicep, casually, almost lazily. Brother Moore laughed and shook it again.

"And down I reach, somehow without knowing why. And he stings me again! He stings me here, and here, and here." Brother Moore pointed to his calf, his elbow, and his forearm. His voice was throaty and thick. His white shirt gleamed. "And without knowing why, I hold him still. I hold him tight. And he hurts me not. He hurts me not! It is a sign!"

"A sign!" A few listeners called back; but there seemed to be a lack of enthusiasm. Up front, some of the women had their hands in the air, catching the Spirit. Leatha was among them, her face luminous, her eyes half closed.

"The serpent bites and hurts me not! Hallelujah!"

"Hallelujah!" came the reply, more voices this time.

"I cast him from me!" Brother Moore shouted, flinging the copperhead in the river with a sweep of his arm. Larry heard a distant splash.

Everyone waited. Brother Moore paused, panting. Larry forced his gaze away from him back to Leatha, feeling the weight of the sinner, the nonbeliever, slowly burden his heart. Even so, he could only watch her with longing. The evening breeze gently rippled her dress.

Brother Moore drew a breath. "But what does it mean? What is the meaning of this sign? What is the portent? What is the message?"

They all waited. Brother Moore gazed up at them. Behind him the quarter moon shone through the trees, spangling the water.

Brother Moore lowered his voice. "We are not of this world, brothers and sisters. We are leaving this old world behind. 'Behold,

I come quickly,' said the Lord, Revelation Twenty-two, seven. We must be ready. We must be strong."

He paused again.

"But not all are ready," he whispered. "Not all are strong."

Larry suddenly felt cold. How could he have known? How could he even have seen him join the crowd? For an instant he thought about slipping down the tree and away. But he decided to stay. See it through, let it happen.

"How do we search out the secret weakness?" Brother Moore said, his voice rising. "Who still belongs to the old world?"

Slowly he lifted the shoebox, which he had been holding by his side. He tilted it toward the group; in the dim light they could see the money. Glances passed.

"The Lord will provide," Brother Moore said. "We will eat of the hidden manna."

Brother Moore tipped the shoebox a little more. A few bills slid out and landed in the river. They eddied around his knees for a moment and then floated away.

"The Lord will provide," crooned Brother Moore. He tipped the shoebox further, sending more money into the river. He stopped; watched the crowd; tilted the box higher.

One man, then another, then two more, bolted from the bank and dashed after the money. Brother Moore dumped out the rest of the box. He stood still, ignoring the men as they thrashed in the water.

One of them called up to the bank, "Go get a flashlight. Go, I tell you!" A woman ran past Larry.

Leatha fell to her knees and began to speak in that strange private language Larry had heard her use in church. She was oblivious to the turmoil around her, men wrestling in the dark water, Brother Moore standing immovable with his arms uplifted, the people on the bank milling restlessly in a mix of prayers, whispered conferences, and uncertain gestures. Larry listened to her voice, sweet and high with a strange rhythm that was not exactly like speech but not not-speech either. It sounded like baby talk, like moon-man talk. But how could he know? He'd never talked to God. Maybe that was God's language.

He clung to his tree and watched. Some of that money was his; but he felt no desire to go after it even though he knew he would be packing his tent and leaving tonight like the men whose attachment to the world had been revealed just now. There was the roll of bills in his pocket, of course. But he felt like tossing it into the river too. No: better keep it for now, divide it up with everyone in a month or two.

"There you have it!" bellowed Brother Moore. "There you have it." The men in the water stopped their fishing and looked up. He turned to them. "Leave our presence. Leave tonight. Take your worldly thoughts with you." The men scrambled up the slippery bank, dripping, trying to catch roots and tufts of grass without losing hold of their money.

"Now everyone, go," Brother Moore said. "I must pray." He tossed the shoebox into the water and walked away from them toward the far bank, his legs sloshing slowly as he reached the deeper water. Everyone began to shuffle toward camp with an air of solemnity that might have passed for embarrassment.

Leatha was the last to leave. In the failing light her countenance shone like a lesser moon, reflecting radiance from some invisible source. Larry slid down from his vantage place and caught her hand as she went by.

For a moment they did not speak. She was breathless, but her expression was serene. She smiled at him, and the words were out of his mouth before he even knew what they were going to be.

"I'm going back to Piedmont tonight. If you want to, I could take you home."

She stared at him. Larry tried to smile.

"I'd like to get married soon. Maybe a couple of weeks, or a month, or something. What do you say?"

She jerked her hand away and covered her mouth. Larry felt repulsive, profane. She darted away.

Everyone was gone. Larry sat down on the trodden grass of the riverbank. He could hear Brother Moore wading through the shallows on the other side. There was a gravel bar out that direction. Pretty soon he would hear his footsteps crunching the gravel. Alone, Larry became aware that the silence was actually full of sounds: insects, breeze, water, faraway voices, his own breathing, the creaking of trees. The air was warm. It would be another foggy night. Larry waited for some thought to enter his mind, but none came just yet. He decided he would sit for a while by the river, sit in the empty dark, sit and not think, just sit and listen to the droning machinery of the exhausted world.

Discussion Questions

The End of the World

1. The belief that the end of the world is near has been held by millions of people throughout history. How might holding this belief change a person's thoughts and actions?

2. Reflecting on his day of judgment, Larry thinks about an incident that happened during his teenage years. Is he being too hard on himself?

3. Larry is ordered by Mr. Brooks to compromise his beliefs. Does he make the right choice?

4. The other characters in this story think of Larry as a weirdo. Do you see similarities between them and him?

5. What do you make of Larry's witnessing around the county, especially the encounter that he remembers as "a personal vision of death"?

Weeds and Wildness

1. The title of this story comes from the poem "Inversnaid" by Gerard Manley Hopkins, which ends with these lines: "What would the world be, once bereft / Of wet and of wildness? Let them be left, / O let them be left, wildness and wet; / Long live

the weeds and the wilderness yet." How do you see this story in relation to those lines?

2. Mark thinks of his family as "not people who spoke of such things." What things do they not speak of? Is his perception true?

3. When the story begins, Mark is feeling aimless and without a clear sense of his future. Is he any different at the end?

4. One thread of the story is the difference in generational outlook between Mark and his grandfather. How are they different? Are they all that different?

5. Max, the camp director, prides himself on knowing how "we handle it out here in the country." If there is such a thing as a country way of doing things, how does it show up in this story?

Why Miss Elizabeth Never Joined the Shakespeare Club

1. This story takes place in the context of small-town social life. But are the issues it raises specific to that setting?

2. The narrator says that in the modern age, "no thought need be kept secret and any deed is acceptable as long as it's sincere." Is she right?

3. What would Shakespeare think of the Shakespeare Club?

4. Many people look to the past nostalgically, with a sense that life used to be simpler and more innocent. Does this story's narrator see the past that way?

5. William Faulkner's story "A Rose for Emily" treads the line between Gothic horror and humor. What similarities and differences do you see between these two stories?

Trio Sonata in C

1. Do you see a theme to Grandpa's reminiscences?

2. How well does Tom understand Elizabeth's frustrations?

3. How does Tom's work as a pilot match his approach to domestic life?

4. When Tom says, "He's already in a home," is he being fair?

5. Does Tom's final action restore order to the house?

From Thee to My Sole Self

1. As with "Weeds and Wildness," this story's title is taken from a poem. In this case, it's Keats' "Ode to a Nightingale." What relevance do you see to that reference?

2. At one point in the story, the narrator says, "We all find our own rats to love." Do you think that's true?

3. This is a story in which every important character has done something wrong. How would you characterize their wrongdoings?

4. What would you say is the tone of this story?

5. What characteristics does this narrator share with the narrator of "Miss Elizabeth"?

The Fair

1. Unlike the other stories in this collection, "The Fair" employs multiple points of view, moving from one character to another. What is the effect of these alternating perspectives?

2. This story includes multiple scenes of parent-child interaction. What common threads/significant differences do you see in these interactions?

3. The fair is an institution that dates back hundreds, if not thousands, of years. How is this choice of setting symbolic?

4. What do these disparate characters have in common besides the fact that they are at the fair?

5. One feature of this story is a divide between older and younger characters. What are some factors creating that divide?

The Trouble with Women

1. What examples of irony do you see in this story?

2. How does it affect your reading experience when the narrating character is morally repugnant?

3. What moments do you find humorous that others might view as offensive?

4. The narrator sometimes misinterprets words, either inadvertently or on purpose. Do his failings of language reveal something deeper in himself?

Bill Burkens and Peter Krull

1. What is it about Bill Burkens' death that intrigues Peter so much?

2. Is it a futile effort to try to understand someone fully?

3. Do you find Peter's final assessment of Bill Burkens persuasive?

4. The more prosaically minded characters of the story also have explanations for Bill Burkens' behavior. Do any of those views add insight?

Magic Kids

1. Why do you think Will calls his disease The Thing?

2. Like Leo Tolstoy's "The Death of Ivan Ilyich," this story presents a character facing his imminent mortality. How do you think that situation affects the characters of the story? If you're familiar with "Ivan Ilyich," you might think of the similarities between the protagonists.

3. What strategies are Mom and Dad using to deal with Will's situation?

4. Will seems curiously indifferent to his fate at some points in the story. Why do you suppose that is?

Late and Soon

1. The title comes from William Wordsworth's sonnet "The World Is Too Much With Us." What significance do you see in that?

2. Belle Prospect represents what some people call the "New Ozarks" – an affluent retirement community, complete with the amenities of suburban life. Do you think of the New Ozarks as part of the "real" Ozarks?

3. Dale Green compares selling real estate to warfare. Does that make sense to you, or is he exaggerating?

4. Belle Prospect has numerous scenic overlooks, emphasizing its placement within the landscape. What do you think of as the iconic landscape of the Ozarks?

Unexplained Aerial Phenomena

1. This story takes up the issue of insider/outsider, belonging/ not belonging. How does that distinction inform the story?

2. The story is similar to "Magic Kids" in that it involves an encounter with something beyond ordinary human comprehension. What do the characters' responses tell you about them?

3. What contrasts do you see between Janine's academic life in Springfield and her experiences in Pine Hill?

4. "Unexplained Aerial Phenomena" touches on issues of the effect of the past on the present, as the phenomenon is somehow connected to a drowned village. How do you interpret that connection?

5. Janine tells Woodrow, "The story matters as much to me as the facts." Does that make sense?

Signs and Wonders

1. This story sees the return of Larry, the protagonist of "The End of the World." Has Larry changed since that story?

2. What prompts Larry's strange behavior when he returns to town?

3. Why is he unable to tell the woman about his congregation's decision?

4. The collection begins with "The End of the World" and ends with "Signs and Wonders," both stories about a character envisioning a coming apocalypse. How do these stories reflect on the stories in between?

5. This story contains a number of Biblical references. Do they hold meaning in a modern-day setting?

Scattered Lights

1. The title of this collection is taken from a line in "Weeds and Wildness." How do you see that image governing the overall collection?

2. These stories are set in the Ozarks. What image of the Ozarks is suggested by these stories?

3. Although the stories are set in the Ozarks, do you see them having wider significance about people and life in general?

Steve Wiegenstein is an Ozarks native, novelist, and scholar who has been passionate about writing since the late 1970s, when he co-founded the literary magazine *Ozark Review* while working as a newspaper reporter. His short fiction has appeared in *Kansas Quarterly*, *Louisiana Literature*, *Southern Humanities Review*, *Elder Mountain*, *Nebraska Review*, *Oxford Magazine*, and other journals.

He is the author of *Slant of Light*, *This Old World*, and *The Language of Trees*. *Slant of Light* was an honorable mention for the David J. Langum Historical Fiction Award in 2012, *This Old World* was a finalist for the M. M. Bennetts Award for Historical Fiction in 2014, and *The Language of Trees* received the Missouri Writers Guild's Walter Williams Major Work Award in 2018.

He is an avid hiker and canoeist who hits the trails and floats the streams of the Ozarks every chance he gets. Steve loves to speak at libraries, civic organizations, and other groups about writing, history, and the environment.

He maintains a blog on which he discusses Ozarks-related topics at https://stevewiegenstein.wordpress.com/.